CHASING JUSTICE

by
Peggy Sue McCullough

This is a work of fiction. Names, characters, places, and incidents either are the product of the author's imagination or are used fictitiously. Any resemblance to actual persons, living or dead, events, or locales is entirely coincidental.

Copyright © 2022 by Peggy Sue McCullough

All rights reserved. No part of this book may be reproduced or used in any manner without written permission of the copyright owner except for the use of quotations in a book review. For more information, address: Peggysuemccullough@yahoo.com

First paperback edition September 2022

Book design by Integrative Ink

ISBN: 978-1-7378010-0-9 (Paperback Edition)
ISBN: 978-1-7378010-1-6 (Ebook Edition)

THIS BOOK IS DEDICATED TO MY SON ALEX

CHASING JUSTICE

CHAPTER 1

It was twenty-eight degrees and falling. The family surrounded the fire while looking out the window. They were cocooned in glowing warmth, searching for the car lights to appear. In the black of night, each desperately prayed for C.W. to come home safely.

Sara's wheezing consumed the room. Sara's father, Sam, and grandmother, Violet, looked at each other in the dim light with no words spoken, their worry deepening as more coughing erupted. Sara was propped up on pillows close to the fire, her cinnamon-golden red hair spread out around her head like a halo. It wasn't difficult to see the dark circles below her eyes, the blue lips, and pale skin.

Sara looked at Sam with eyes brighter than sapphires. She smiled as she peered over the heavy blanket that swallowed her. Sam lovingly returned the smile.

"Sam, what's taking him so long?" Violet had been pacing the floor intermittently for the last four hours. She felt sick to her stomach from worry. "What if he's dead?" As soon as the thought surfaced, she shook her head and forced it aside. Weeks would pass, and there would be no word from C.W. No telephone calls. They always feared the worst.

"It's midnight, and the shooting went down at 5 p.m." Sam patted Violet's hand, knowing she was distraught.

Violet knew Sam was trying to console her. He had treated her like a mother since the day they'd met. Actually, the day he'd asked to marry Pearl. Such a happy day. Violet thought of the most precious thing she owned, and it was from Sam—a flowered handkerchief for Mother's Day. It was in a satin container, along with the most beautiful message of sincere love.

With spirit calm as the summer sea moving in sweet serenity, I am sure there is no other in all the world like you, MOTHER.

Violet's love for Sam was for the son she'd never had. They had weathered many a storm together. His words brought her back to the present.

"He probably took the back roads out of Chicago. After all, it was a shooting with multiple victims. You know the cops will want to know where he is, but the boys won't tell them anything. They would never double cross C.W. If anything had happened to him, Sullivan would have called me by now."

The news bulletin at 5 p.m. stated that two armed men sauntered into Sara's Pub in north Chicago, leaving seven dead. It was described as a bloodbath, which didn't leave much to the imagination. It sure did contribute to their anxiety, though.

The card game stopped. All you could hear was the game on the TV in the background. The armed man at the door calmly waved his gun at the money on the table. The regulars in the bar were some tough guys with a lot of violent history behind them. They didn't move. Each was looking to Sullivan for direction.

The intruder pulled his fedora down farther over his eyes and sized up the room. The oldest player at the table, Sullivan, was C.W.'s right-hand man. Dressed in striped slacks and a white shirt with rolled up sleeves, he stood.

"What do you boys need?"

"All your money and the cases of booze in the back room. There's a truck in the back alley, and your boys are going to load it."

Sullivan was contemplating what to do. He looked around. His boys would definitely die. The intruders were armed and itching for a fight. They were restless.

Sullivan suddenly made his move and dove under the card table. The boys at the door fired their .45 caliber semiautomatics, and the players were down to one. The back spray hit the television and the boys who had been watching the game. Now, there was silence. Seven were dead. Customers were huddled anywhere they could hide. Two of the dead were C.W.'s henchmen.

C.W. was behind the hidden panel checking in the new liquor shipment. He was on full alert when the gunfire started. He cautiously cracked the hidden panel that was located five feet behind and to the left of the intruders. C.W.'s eyes shifted, calculating the number of armed men. As C.W. entered the gunfight, the intruder spun around toward him. Both had their guns out and were firing. Three loud shots rang out. The intruder went down and stayed down. Blood poured from his head. C.W. dove to the plank floor and shot the second intruder without hesitation.

When it was over, C.W.'s customers began crawling out from under tables and from behind the bar. "Sullivan, the cops will be here in fifteen minutes," C.W. yelled. "I've not been here. I'm out of town. Anyone who doesn't want to be questioned, get out of here now."

Eight of the remaining customers ran for the front door, and two, for the alley. Three men stayed to support the alibi to protect the business. C.W. handed his gun to Sullivan and went to retrieve another for the road.

"I got this, boss. Get out of here. We've been through this before," said Sullivan.

"I'll call you in a few days. You know where I'll be. You know what to say. It was self-defense. Tell the boys how to respond. Ask for an attorney if it goes that far." C.W. put a different pistol in his waistband and bolted for the alley door. His black sedan roared to life and tires squealed as he left the alley and headed for the farm.

CHAPTER 2

One hour later, on the outskirts of Chicago, C.W. finally relaxed. He was thinking about Sara when he noticed blood seeping and spreading onto his shirt sleeve. In all the gun play, he hadn't realized he'd been hit.

It looked like it was just a scratch. He took a handkerchief and tied it tightly to stop the bleeding. Violet could fix him up. She had many years of experience stitching up the neighbors and delivering babies.

He couldn't wait to see Sara. She was like his own daughter, but she was Sam's. He had spent more time on the farm than the pub when Sam went to war. Sam was the closest thing to a brother he would ever have. C.W. had made a promise to Sam to take care of Violet and his wife, Pearl. Sara was born while Sam was at war. Since C.W. couldn't do much four hours away in Chicago, he stayed at the farm for weeks at a time. He farmed, worked the garden, and held Pearl's hand, telling her Sam would be home soon and everything would be okay.

In the back of his mind, C.W. thought about a life at the farm instead of in Chicago at the pub. *We all have to make our own mistakes*, C.W. thought, sighing. Things just didn't work out that way.

Then the baby was born, and Pearl had complications. Violet had delivered Sara. Her midwife experience was invaluable. Pearl was shivering, and he piled on the blankets while Violet assisted with the baby.

Violet took Sara and cleaned her ever so gently. C.W. saw first-hand the total love for someone else. Sara was five pounds, eight ounces and perfectly formed. The bridge of her nose was tiny and almost flat. Her lips were beautiful. She had ten little toes and ten little fingers. She was perfect. The first time he held her, he knew something had happened. At that moment, C.W. knew what perfect true love was. He realized he had never experienced it before in his life. C.W. held Sara ever so gently and marveled at her beauty. Sam had already asked him to be Sara's godfather. He promised to protect her until the day he died.

Snow had come the night before, covering the farm with a white blanket. The branches were all heavy and laden with snow. The lane to the house was packed with three-foot drifts. There was no way in or out.

The red stain on Pearl's nightgown became brighter and spread. She was clammy and pale. Violet quickly laid the baby down to tend to her daughter. Violet massaged her uterus to help it contract and lessen the bleeding. Dr. Gerstein had been notified the minute Pearl went into labor, but it was doubtful he would get through the snow drifts. C.W. was more scared watching her decline than if he were in a gun fight. He was as helpless as that new baby.

It was six hours before Dr. Gerstein arrived. He had called in a favor from one of his patient's husbands who had a road grader. He had been picked up at his house, and he and Mark had made their way south of town and one mile east at the crossroads. Dr. Gerstein didn't slow down when he hit the doors. He did hug Violet in passing.

Immediately he prepared an intravenous solution to combat the blood loss. Dr. Gerstein inserted the needle in Pearl's vein and secured it. He looked at Violet, who also looked pale and exhausted.

6

After the needle was secured, he went and put his arms around Violet again. She was crying from the fear of possibly losing Pearl, and no one could help her. It was a relief to have Doc show up and support her.

Pearl grew weaker each day and eventually passed after Sam got home from the war. It was the most devastating day of his life. C.W. grieved beside Sam for weeks.

I don't need to be thinking about this right now, C.W. told himself.

CHAPTER 3

C.W. knew Sara's Pub would be fine. Lawmen in Chicago were offered a lot of money to look the other way. If that didn't work, a convincing threat went a long way, too. Yes, the pub was named after a child. C.W. was often asked who Sara was. He would just smile and say, "It's who I always go home to and always will." Some women didn't really care for that because they assumed it was another woman.

Through the years, the pub had been a speakeasy and brewery. It had fake wall panels that led to the back alley and trap doors that hid the booze C.W. provided to the greater hotels of Chicago. Bodyguards with plenty of firepower were always throughout the pub. There was illegal gambling and sport-book operations most nights.

C. W. pulled into the farm. Sam and Violet saw the car lights at the same time and jumped up.

"Thank God he's here," Sam yelled, grabbing his coat and running for the door. He headed for the stand-alone garage and opened the double doors. As Sam opened the car door, he saw the blood.

"C.W., are you hit?"

"It's minor, Sam. Just a scratch."

"Okay, we'll see. Let's get you inside and let Violet check it out. I'll come back out and get the blood out of the car."

Violet was standing by the door waiting on them. The quaking in her legs had subsided. She reached to hug him. "Oh my God, C.W. Are you shot?" Now, she was shaking again. "I'll call Doc."

"No, don't call Doc. You can fix me up fine. The wound's not bad. Just a flesh injury. You can fix me up in nothing flat."

"Well, I wanted to hug you, but now I think I need to beat you." They all laughed.

"C.W., you have to quit this gangster nonsense. You're going to get killed, and then what will we do?"

"Now, Violet, you know we all got to go some time. Right? Without me, what would you do for excitement?"

"Smartass. You know we live our lives through you. Let's go to the utility room and let me get you fixed up. Sara doesn't need to see you all bloody. She's under the weather this week. Having trouble breathing again."

"For God's sake, Violet, why don't you and Sam bring her to Chicago to see a specialist?"

"You know we trust Dr. Gerstein, and he is here every week checking on her and changing her medications."

"Yes, I know he loves to see you, too, Violet. He's a little sweet on you."

"Sam, get a shirt for him and a clean pair of pants. Hush up, C.W. I need to get this sutured. You ready?"

"Yes, ma'am. Let's get it over with."

Sam headed for the door after he dropped a pair of pants and shirt on the chair. "Violet, where is the peroxide? I need to clean the car. The blood is on the seat and door."

Violet handed him the peroxide and a bottle of cleaning solution, too.

C.W. went to see Sara once he was sutured and cleaned up. She was sleeping on the floor in the living room by the fire. He knelt and kissed her. She looked so frail as the firelight danced around them.

He sat down in the rocking chair. Sam joined them.

"The car is clean. There was a lot of blood. You sure you feel okay, C.W?"

"Oh yes. I'm good now. This is small beans compared to some of my escapades." He chuckled.

Sara stirred and looked around. She saw C.W., got up, and put her arms around his neck, kissing him on the cheek. She was wheezing.

"Whoever is in the rocking chair has to rock me. It helps me breathe better."

"It would be an honor." C.W. opened his arms, and she sat on his lap. Her head resting in the nape of his neck made him hug her closer. She drew her long legs up into his lap. He loved everything about her.

"Are you having more breathing problems?"

"Yes, I went to Pearline's yesterday and walked by the creek. I heard a branch snap and thought someone was behind me, so I took off running. There wasn't any place to hide, so I ran farther down the creek to the bend. I saw vines hanging from the trees, which I have swung on before. It was still a long way to reach them. I was already short of breath, but the farther I ran, the more my chest tightened. Probably because of the cold air. I started wheezing more when I heard something crashing through the branches. I knew I couldn't outrun anyone, but I could see the vines. I grabbed the first one I got to and pushed with my feet and body with all the energy I had left. I arched my body and sailed through the air, clearing the fence and the creek. Wheee!" She laughed and coughed at the same time. C.W. patted her on the back.

"When I landed, I ran like the devil was after me. I saw Dad on the tractor in the field, so I crossed the road, climbed the bank, and waved my hands. Dad saw me and turned the tractor around. We both saw a boy with black hair climbing out of the creek just looking at us. I was scared. Pearline didn't even know I was behind her house, or she would have come to help me. I guess that's what made me sicker."

"What the hell's going on, Sam? Who was the kid in the creek?"

Sara couldn't see Sam, as her back was to him. Sam put his finger to his lips, telling C.W. they would talk later.

"I'm trying to figure out who it was," Sam replied. "Not sure yet. Sara, tell C.W. about the information Grandma is gathering to help get you better."

"Grandma is writing a paper on me. Every day she writes what the weather is. She includes if we're farming, wind blowing, and dust in the air. She notes if herbicides are being sprayed on the field, pollen factors, and a hundred other things. She also writes down everything I eat. She and Doc are trying to figure out what makes me have breathing problems." Her coughing now sounded like a bark.

"Well, you definitely need to eat more. I told Violet I would find a doctor in Chicago if we need to."

"I'll be okay. Dr. Gerstein says I have allergies and asthma. That's why Grandma's writing down everything. I go to the chiropractor now, too. He gives me hot treatments on my chest. He uses a great big machine on me, and I sweat. It does make me feel better. It takes an hour to drive to the doctor's office, and the treatment is another hour. Then, we have to drive home. I'm really tired after the treatments. So, what kind of trouble are you in tonight?" she asked, abruptly changing the subject.

"Well, girl, listen to you. Do you think I only come to see you when I'm in trouble?"

"Yes and no. I heard the news tonight, so yes. I knew you'd be here. Grandma and Dad have paced for hours. They were ecstatic when you pulled in. I wasn't really asleep." Sara smiled at C.W. "We love you being here. Actually, I'm the luckiest girl in the world to have you. All the excitement in your life keeps us going. Now, would you do your job and rock me, please?"

C.W. smiled. "Yes, ma'am, I will rock all night and love every minute of it. You know that pretty soon, you will be too big to rock. Actually, you may already be there." He squeezed her tight and chuckled. Sara was lying on his bandaged arm, but he had never felt better with Sara there on his lap. Sam and Violet just shook their heads.

Violet stood up. "It has been a long day. I'm heading for bed. Sara, you head for bed in just a while after you get your fill of rocking." They all laughed. "C.W., you sleep in Sara's room tonight. She will be in my room until she is better. It's too cold in the old farmhouse. You can get it warmed up tomorrow."

C.W. nodded his head in agreement to the sleeping arrangements.

Sara went to bed about thirty minutes after Grandma did. "I'll see you tomorrow, won't I, C.W.?"

"Yes, I will be here with bells on just to see you." He smiled at Sara, and she just laughed.

After Sara left, C.W. turned to Sam. "What's with the treatment Sara's getting. Is it safe? And who the hell is the kid she saw? What's going on?"

"It helps her, C.W. It's ultrasound deep heat treatments. We had to do something. It increases circulation, and she does feel better. As far as the boy goes, I think I know who the kid is. You remember Medlar, who lives down the hill? You know who I'm talking about. You did a lot of bootlegging with him years ago. Well, he had a kid. Seems about the right age for who I saw. You probably saw him when he was a young child. Well, now he's back."

"Back from where?" C.W. asked.

"Oh, it's a long story. We'll talk about it in the morning. I have to get some shut-eye. I have to clear the roads early in the morning, and it's already midnight," Sam replied.

CHAPTER 4

C.W. was there for breakfast. He was a few years younger than her dad. Together, they were a force to deal with; they stuck together through thick and thin.

Sara picked up on their conversations. They were guarded and spoke in code, but she understood all of it. The local paper was often referring to and reporting on the "Gang." There were articles on bootlegging, mobsters, gambling, gaming joints, raids, and gun battles with bloodbaths in Chicago. Sara knew how to read between the lines of her father and C.W.'s gibberish.

C.W. always carried a .44 revolver, and other guns were in the shop, corncrib, garage, and Grandma's old house at the back of the farm. She planned to crawl under the house in the crawlspace if any gunfire started. C.W. had his personal arsenal. Sara just liked to explore and had found them. The pistol she found in the henhouse and the outhouse were carrying things a little too far. She'd give him hell on that at a later time.

Sara finished reading the newspaper. "Sounds like you made the front page, C.W. Must have been a shootout to remember."

C.W. playfully grabbed the paper and glanced at it.

"What makes you think that article is about me? I don't see my name anywhere."

"Really, C.W. I'm smarter than the average bear, and this is you they are talking about."

Violet laughed. "Give it up, C.W. She's too old to fool anymore."

C.W. looked at Sara. "Yes, that is about me. Just remember there's two sides to every story, and then there is the truth. If you want the truth, you will always hear it from me."

"I'm not sure all those details are appropriate now. Maybe someday when Sara is older. Your lifestyle might be hard to understand," Sam said.

"My life is unique. Some might think I rationalize my decisions. I just live to take from the rich mobsters to give to the ones I love and to the poor. I'm always going to help the less fortunate. I just do it in an unorthodox way. No one can say how much longer I will live on the edge. Not even me. When the day comes, it will be fast and furious, and I will walk away in the blink of an eye."

C.W. pushed his chair back from the table and looked out multiple windows of the old farmhouse. He scanned the cornfield—always watching and listening. He knew how to avoid a trap.

"Sam and Violet, I won't involve you if the law ever comes here. I'll say I held you at gunpoint. Or I'll say someone told me Violet could suture me up. I have a lot of enemies. Rest assured, I never let anyone follow me to the place and people I love most."

Violet laughed. "After all these years, do you really think we're worried about any of that? We really thought you would outgrow all of these shenanigans. Boy, were we wrong!"

Sam just shook his head—fearing the day the newspaper would reveal C.W.'s demise. Sam fought the urge to say something more. He didn't want to admit when and if that day came, it would devastate him.

Sara walked to C.W. "Well, if we're by the outhouse and I'm in it when one of your enemies get here, you'd better be able to catch well. I'm going to toss you a weapon from the outhouse or the

14

henhouse, and then I'm going to run like hell to one of my ten hid-ing spots—and neither are the outhouse or henhouse." The laughter erupted from everyone.

"You rascal. You're too smart for your own good. Don't worry. I accept that offer, and believe me, I will catch that gun you toss."

"I know you will. You'd better get your shoulder holster on, C.W. I know you have to carry it while you're here. Those snakes are really bad—NOT." Sarah teased C.W.

"Okay, girl. You'd better quit while you're ahead or still got one."

Sara took off running and C.W. followed, laughing as he chased her. When he caught her, he swirled her in the air. "You'd better be nice to me." He pulled his hat down farther. He always wore the same hat Sam wore and dressed identical. Their physique was similar, and he could pass for Sam easily when on the tractor or working outside. They went to the garage together to look at the car.

C.W. opened the driver's side. "Good job, Sam. Not a speck of blood anywhere."

"Right. You need to come farm with me and give this mob life up before it's too late," Sam remarked.

"I know, I know," C.W. replied. "It is so exciting, and the re-wards are a thrill."

Sam just looked at him.

C.W. stayed on the farm for two weeks. He often slept at Vio-let's old house at the back of the farm. It still contained a lot of her belongings when her and Ezra lived there. She just couldn't part with them. C.W. liked being in a house with good memories. He had spent a lot of his younger years right here in this house. He was just a ghost that came and went. One day, he would leave suddenly. No one could predict how long he would be gone. Then, he would return.

C.W. had grown up on the very country roads surrounding the farm. He knew the lay of the land and the hiding spots. Some of those hiding spots were so close to the sheriff's office, he could have touched them and watched every move they made. Others were tucked away so far no one could find his refuge. If it were a planned visit, he came like Dapper Dan. He was suited up, shiny shoes, fedora hats, and jewelry. He looked like a famous gangster. Bottom line, he *was* famous. The next day, he was dressed to work.

Sam loved having C.W. on the farm to help him. He lived the excitement of C.W.'s life through the stories of encounters with the law, his escapes, gin, fights, and gambling. Of course, he couldn't forget the women.

C.W. made a mistake that next visit, when he invited Sam to come to Chicago and see his pub. They were at the supper table when he asked, and what happened devastated everyone.

"Sam, why don't you take a week and come see the pub? I'll introduce you to the boys."

Anger pushed through Sara with such violence, she scared herself. Shaking, she jumped up from the table so fast the wooden chair toppled over, hitting the floor at the same time she slammed her fist on the table. The dishes rattled and bounced. "You are NOT going to Chicago to be identified with C.W. and his mob activities. You are NOT leaving me an orphan. How dare you think of yourself and leave us here alone to go live that dangerous life? That would be the end of everything." Sara was shouting by this time. "If you go, I will find a way to Chicago, and I will follow you. I know the address to the tavern."

Violet stood and tried to reach out to Sara as the tears ran down her face. C.W. hung his head, and Sam was speechless. Sara slammed the front screen door as she left and was gone until dark. The house was silent. All three had busied themselves with tasks but were really looking for Sara. Going to Chicago was never brought up again.

Sara walked across the neighbor's fields for miles that day—a time for thinking and a lot of crying. The fear of her and Violet being left to fend for themselves was overwhelming. She went to a deserted barn and set in the loft for hours just thinking about how their life would change if Sam left and just happened to get into trouble with C.W. After all, C.W. was always in trouble. "What would we do? Would we lose the farm? What if Grandma got sick?"

Sara came in at dark and sat down where everyone was in front of the TV.

"I'm sorry," she said. "I just can't deal with this. The possibilities are overwhelming for me."

C.W. stood and pulled her up from the couch. He placed his arms around her. "I understand, and it will never be brought up again. I'm sorry. I wouldn't hurt you for anything."

Violet took Sara's hand. "Your dad would never leave us, sweetheart."

Sara shook her head.

Sam wrapped his arms around Sara. "That is C.W.'s life. I made my choice years ago. I love you, your grandma, and the farm. Please don't worry about this anymore. Okay?"

Again, Sara nodded her head yes.

C.W. had farmed years ago but found out he could make more money bootlegging. Fact is, old man Medlar was a main contact years ago, and he was only a quarter of a mile down the road to the east in front of Sam's property. C.W. did not respect the law and settled issues with guns and violence. He knew all the back roads and ran liquor for years. Then, he headed for St. Louis some years back with four loads of liquor, which he had taken by force. His enterprise in St. Louis made him a fortune, along with his dirty dealings.

The era of "Terrific Bucket Trade" made him even wealthier. That five o'clock whistle blew, and every kid headed for home to retrieve their dad's beer bucket and ten cents. The kids would race for the bar, throw the bucket on the counter, get it filled, and race home so the beer would be waiting for Dear Old Dad when he got off work. What a set-up. Officials were paid off if needed, so the illegal sales could continue unimpeded.

C.W. had set up code names and peepholes to further the sales and eliminate major issues with the law. The fact that he was young and reckless kept him wild and crazy. He had knocked over multiple gambling joints and gotten quite the reputation. Most of the cops left him alone. C.W. moved his dealings to Chicago when things got hot—too many killings, even though they were self-defense. There was no proof of his involvement in any shootouts. No arrests, and his record always came up clean. Only by the grace of God, and he knew it.

CHAPTER 5

"Grandma, I'm going to go to Pearline's a while," Sara yelled, as she headed for the door. She grabbed her sweater from the chair and slid it on.

"Wait. Let me call her and tell her you are coming. I'll walk you to the mailbox, and Pearline can walk to the crossroads so she can see you. You call when you are starting back, and I will go to the mailbox and wait on you. That boy scared me. Be back by one o'clock."

"Okay, Grandma." Sara went out the front door and kicked the kickstand up on her bike. She waited for Grandma to make her call and get her shoes on. Violet got her jacket and slid the gun in the deep pocket. She felt the gun's cold, hard steel as she slid her hand in her pocket. No more chances, was all she thought about. Sara coasted down the driveway until she had to turn on the gravel road.

"Sara, you tell Pearline hello and to come for dinner Sunday, and we'll catch up on family news."

"I'll tell her, Grandma."

Sara was very cautious when she got to the gravel road, even if it was just a quarter of a mile. Lots of cars at times. Some drivers came from Medlar's place and were liquored up.

Sara felt like someone was watching her. As she approached the crossroads, she saw Pearline standing there waving.

Johnny was well hidden in the tree line. He lay on his belly and watched as Sara rode her bicycle towards him. He noticed her grandmother right behind her. That was odd. Then, he saw the neighbor walking down the gravel road to meet her. There was no way he could get close to her today.

Johnny just wanted to talk to Sara. He knew he'd scared her when he chased her through the creek. She had been nice to him the first years of school. He would talk to her on the bus. He remembered the other kids laughing at him and making fun of his clothes. Sara had stood up for him.

Johnny closed his eyes as he shook his head. The voices were back. He was struggling to decide which voice he should follow. Which message was the right one? He wanted to be close to Sara, but the next voice said to touch her and take her to her knees. He mentally told the voices to stop and shook his head again, thinking it would make the voices go away. She had been a friend once, but that was so long ago. He didn't have any friends now. The voices were not always trustworthy. One minute the voice would be kind, then the next minute it would tell him to kill or hurt someone.

He slid backwards, losing sight of the road, and headed to his house.

"Hi, Pearline. What are you doing today?"

"I was hoping you would come to visit. How's your grandma?"

"Everybody is good. I'm bored and need a book fix."

"Well, I think I can fix you up. How about some milk and fresh peanut butter cookies before you head for the attic?"

"I'd love some. Your petunias are beautiful. I love purple flowers."

"When you finish, I'll show you the garden. The tomatoes are beautiful. I'll send a pie home with you. I have way too many peaches and had to bake and can all day yesterday."

"I love peaches. Dad and Grandma do, too. Grandma wants you to come to Sunday dinner. Can you?"

"Of course. I can come to dinner Sunday."

After seeing the garden, Sara climbed the stairs to the attic and sat in front of the old wood bookcase. She started pulling and reading a few lines to see what she wanted to read. Romance was boring. Eventually, she found two mysteries and took them to the feather bed. She lay there and read for an hour, then went back downstairs. "I'd better get home before Grandma comes down and gets me. Can you call and tell her I am headed home? She wants to meet me at the mailbox."

"Why is she meeting you? She never has before."

"Well, last week I was in the creek behind your house and a boy with black hair scared me. He was chasing me, and I was able to use the vines to get away and get back to the field where Dad was. Now, they're keeping an eye on me. Have you ever seen a boy hanging around here?"

Pearline said, "No." She *had* seen the boy, but she wasn't about to scare Sara any more than she already was. She would talk to Sam about it.

"Well, you just call me whenever you want to come down. Let me call Violet right now, before you get on your bike. I'll meet you even closer to your house until we figure this out. You be careful. I'll watch you until you get to your driveway."

Pearline hugged Sara and watched until she hit the long lane. Pearline loved having Sara visit a few hours every week. Pearline's son married, but never had children. Sara was like her own.

When Sara got to her room, she peeled off her socks and shoes. She went to the bathroom and peered at herself. *Why would anyone chase me?* she thought. *I'm skinny as a rail. I have dark circles under my eyes all the time, and my red hair is all over the place.* As she stared, she saw her eyes as a sea of blue. Her skin was flawless, and maybe her red hair didn't look that bad. She definitely needed bigger boobs. She saw an impish smile as she looked at herself. Sara

21

threw on her PJ's, fluffed her pillow, and hugged it tightly. She was fast asleep in seconds.

Sara jumped off the last step on the bus. She walked the lane surrounded with high banks and wildflowers. The trees lined both side of the banks. The tall field of cornstalks hid her from the house that sat on high ground and Granny's watchful eye. The white sheets flapped in the wind behind the old, white wood farmhouse. Sara stopped dead in her tracks. There was no mistaking someone was behind the house just inside the cornfield. A younger boy was squatted down and scanning the farm. Grandma was in the garden hoeing weeds and didn't see the stranger. He was very thin and taller than Sara. He was dressed in black shirts and pants, which matched his raven hair. He was pale—almost ghostly. It was the same boy.

Johnny was watching for Sara every day now. The voices wouldn't stop. He had to get close to her. He wanted to look into her eyes and touch her. It was time to right all wrongs. He heard Sara scream for her grandmother. The voices were whispering in his head. She's here, somewhere. He stood, trying to see where she'd hid.

"Grandma, Grandma, come quick," Sara screamed at the top of her lungs as she ran up the lane. Violet ran for the house at the same time she saw movement at the corner of her vision. The boy had stood and was trying to see where Sara was. Sara was crouched by the low brick wall at the front of the house where the steps led to the front door. Sara saw Grandma running.

"I'm here," Sara shouted.

Grandma reached down and pulled her up to go in the house. "Thank God you're all right. You scared me to death. I saw Johnny. That's what you were yelling for, isn't it?" Violet took the shotgun from behind the door and loaded it. She then went to the window where she had seen Johnny, but he was long gone.

"Yes, I haven't seen him for a long time. He looks different. I would never have guessed who he was. It's the same boy that was in the creek."

Johnny saw them run for the house. The voices were yelling now. They called him stupid. That black hole opened in his mind to the million times his father had called him the same thing. Stupid. He was on the edge, trying to decide what to do.

He looked away from the house. His thoughts went to how she would be soft when he touched her. Her legs were long and slender. She had grown up since he had last seen her. He was going to have to work harder to get close to her. Now, they knew he was back and watching.

Violet went straight to the phone and called Sheriff Bone. "Michael, this is Violet. The Medlar boy is creeping us out. He was on the property today and scared both Sara and me. Just hiding in the cornfield and watching. We weren't aware he was back from the boys' farm."

"Yes, I'll stop by his dad's place this afternoon and have a talk with him. I'm sorry I didn't let you know he had been released when his dad got out of prison early."

That evening, Violet shared with Sam that Johnny had been on the property.

Sam was angry and feared for Violet and Sara's safety. He went out after dinner in the dusk and walked. He looked over the property, searching for movement. He saw no one.

Two days later, Sara stepped off the bus steps and saw her father standing at the edge of the cornfield above the gravel road with Johnny and an old, haggard man. Her father swept his hand over the cornfield and put a finger close to the boy's face, as though warning him of something. Then, he forcefully pushed the boy in the chest, causing the boy to stagger backward. Sara continued to walk the lane. She was sure they'd heard the bus. Maybe not. It was a pretty heated discussion going on in the cornfield. She wasn't visible at the bottom of the bank, so she climbed to the edge of the bank so she could see better.

Sam yelled, "If you come near my family again, I will kill you. I thought maybe both of you would like to right some old wrongs. Maybe, be a good neighbor. Haven't either of you learned a damn thing while you've been away?"

Johnny sneered. "I've just begun to create hell in your lives, and I'm nowhere near done. I remember how your daughter kicked me the night you took me to your house. Why couldn't I have stayed with you? But, no. You had to call the sheriff, and I was taken to The Boys Ranch. It was hell every day and night. Maybe Sara needs to experience some of what I was subjected to. She sure has grown up and is purty."

Sam's right arm was so fast, neither Johnny nor his dad expected it. With one quick jab, the boy was out cold, lying on the gravel. Sam had been the best boxer in his platoon during his army career and had made quite a name for himself. He had taught boxing for two years to the young enlisted. The old man stepped back and didn't say a word. Not that he said much anyway. Sam probably hadn't heard anything good ever come from Bart's mouth. He was always hostile and berating people.

Bart turned and slowly walked down the road to his dilapidated house. Johnny was left on the road. Sam turned as well. He climbed on the tractor and drove to the corncrib to unwind. He was dangerously angry.

Sara quickly slid down the bank and ran for the house. She wondered what it was he had been subjected to. Why would Johnny want her to experience it? Sara caught a whiff of the lilac bush that sat beside the steps. She took them two at a time.

Sara went in the back door, slammed her books on the table, and sat down. Then, she ran back to the screen door and hooked the lock. She picked up the newspaper. The headlines read, "Jake Medlar released from prison after murdering his wife." Sarah said out loud, "Welcome home. Looks like both father and son are back, and I need to learn to shoot. C.W. looks like the man for the job. It's going to be a hell of a summer."

Violet had heard that comment and went to the table. "What's going on? You seem a little out of sorts, and why do you need to learn to shoot all of a sudden?"

"Well, wouldn't you? I'm having a bad day. I see that old man Medlar is back, and I know Johnny is chasing me. Now, Dad hits Johnny and knocks him out cold. Mr. Medlar was with Johnny and didn't do anything. Just walked off and left Johnny on the road. It's been a hell of a day."

Violet only got out a "What!" in response to Sara's declaration before Sam walked in. The door slammed behind him, shaking the house. He headed straight for the bathroom. He washed his face and hands, running his fingers through his hair. Sam went to the table and sat down. His face was taught and muscles, tense. He could sense they knew what had happened.

"I apologize for my behavior, but I am tired of this boy, and I will not have it any longer. He has been warned, and now I will take charge of this matter."

No one said a word. They were both smart enough to know when Sam had had enough.

Sam rose from the table and went directly to the phone. The conversation was one-sided, but it was obvious Sam was speaking with C.W.

CHAPTER 6

C.W. arrived two days later. Sara was under the apple tree when he pulled in. It was a sunny Saturday morning. Sam walked to C.W.'s car. They opened the back door and were doing something for about ten minutes. Then, a beautiful white German Shepherd came bounding from the back seat. It was astounding to look at. It had fine lines and a muscular, powerful body.

C.W. gave a command to sit, and it sat. Then, he said heel, and the dog fell into step on C.W.'s left side. C.W. had gotten the dog six months ago, but he had been training it and making sure it was dependable.

Sara jumped up and ran to the car. "Wow. What a dog. I didn't know you had a dog, C.W."

C.W. hugged Sara and swung her around. "Oh my gosh, Sara. You've grown six inches and put on some weight." He feigned back pain, putting his hand on his back. "OOOOh—my back."

Sara laughed, and Sam was smiling. "Knock it off, C.W. It'll take a lot more than me to get you down." Sara playfully slapped at his arm.

"Sara, meet your dog and shake." The dog lifted a paw and extended it. Sara was smiling ear-to-ear and extended her hand.

"Oh my gosh. I can't believe it. Is it a he or she? Can I hug her or touch her?"

"It's a girl. You can touch her. Let her get used to you. What will you name her?"

"She's so beautiful and truly a sight to see. I'll have to think about it. A strong name is so important." Sara was jumping up and down, and the dog just cocked its head.

"This is a K-9 trained police dog, Sara," said C.W. "She is trained to patrol, scale a wall, and enter a vehicle and hold down occupants. It will attack on command and be vicious or gentle. She is the best of the best. Most other German Shepherds are brown and black. Since she is white, the K-9 trainer allowed me to take her. Believe it or not, I actually have a friend on the police force. I brought her for you. But, Sara, a dog is a big responsibility. You have to feed her, and you are responsible for her and how she is to other people. I will show you the commands this week."

"How did you keep her from taking you in, C.W.? You're quite the slippery character."

"Not funny, Sara. I'd hate to have to spank you for having a smart mouth."

"Well, the joke's on you. Now, I can teach her to take you down." Sara was laughing as the two men just shook their heads.

As the week progressed, Sara thought about names. She took the dog down lover's lane to the cemetery and through the bare fields. The plum and peach trees were bare now. Sara was telling her everything about the trees and the farms, just like she was human. Sam and C.W. were watching her and the dog. Sara walked over to them, the dog beside her. They were two peas in a pod from that day on.

"I've decided on a majestic name. Since I can't call her 'The Queen of Sheba,' I will call her Sheba."

"That is a good name," C.W. said.

"I like it," Sam agreed. Sam knew Sheba would protect Sara. God knows she was going to need all the help she could get with Johnny around.

Violet came out about that time and sat down under the shade of the beautiful old maple tree. Sheba walked over and put her head in Violet's lap. "You're a ham. You know where your bread is buttered, and that I'm the chief cook around here. You look hungry. I swear Sheba is smiling." They laughed and loved on Sheba.

Sheba was glued to Sara after that day. She walked Sara to the bus and was waiting on her to get home. Willis, Sara's best friend, admired Sara's new dog from the window of the bus. "Sara, Sheba is a fine dog," Willis commented.

"Isn't she the best? She is good company for Grandma while I'm at school." They watched Sheba until the bus passed the crossroads. If Sara rode her bike, Sheba trotted beside her. She slept either with Sara or on the floor beside her bed every night.

A week later, Sara heard something outside her window and saw a shadow pass. She put her hand on Sheba's muzzle and rolled to the floor. The window was up, and the screen was in. Sara crawled to the living room window and peered back at her bedroom window, her eyes adjusting to the dark. Johnny stood there, trying to get the screen out. Sara walked back to her room with Sheba at her side. She looked at Sheba and pointed to the window and then her hands. As Johnny removed the screen, Sara gave the command, "Attack."

Sheba jumped to the bed and through the open window. Her teeth clamped on Johnny's left hand as they fell back to the ground. The flesh was torn open, and Sara heard a snap as Sheba continued to hold her grip.

Johnny screamed. "Get off me. Call your damn dog." Then, Johnny was erratically punching at Sheba with his free hand as he got his footing. Sheba didn't let go. At that point, Sam and Violet ran into the bedroom. Sam had his .45 in hand and was hanging out the window.

Sara commanded, "Sheba, come." Sheba released and kept barking as a warning. Sam fired at Johnny's left foot as he yelled, "It's over, Johnny. Now, I'm coming after you."

Johnny was trying to crawl away, shrieking in pain. His bloody hand looked distorted.

"I told you I would kill you if you touched my family. That's the only warning shot you will ever get. Next time, it will be to kill, not maim."

Sam went to the phone and called Sherriff Bone. "Michael, I need to report an intruder. Johnny was over here tonight trying to remove the screen from Sara's room. He tried to chase Sara last week, and he's watching us all the time. I'm not sure if my shots got him or not, but I know our dog tore his hand up pretty bad. He was crawling away."

"I'll get dressed and go out there now. Sam, this kid is a problem," replied Sheriff Bone. "He's not been out of the Boys' Ranch even a month, and already he's trying to hurt Sara. I think he's after revenge. I'll stop by in the morning and check on you and Sara. I know I'm going to have to take him in. This won't stop."

"Sara, are you all right?" Sam asked, with genuine concern.

"Absolutely, I'm fine. I think I handled that well. Sheba was my protector, and I told her to attack him."

Sam just looked at her. For a second time, Sara was aware that someone wanted to hurt her. "Johnny has been watching the house to know what room I'm in. We need to keep the blinds pulled down." Sam and Violet just nodded. Worry was written all over their faces.

Sheriff Bone called around 10 a.m. "Sam, I couldn't find anyone at the house. I'll try again tomorrow."

"Okay, we'll keep our eyes open and keep Sara close to us. Thanks."

Johnny was the topic of discussion the next day at breakfast. C.W. was present, but he had missed everything by staying at

Violet's house at the back of the property. Sara was quieter than usual.

"You'll be okay, Sara. I'll see to it," C.W. stated.

They were quiet for a while. Violet looked at Sara. "Five years ago, Mae, old man Medlar's wife, came crawling up our lane. Of course, I helped her in when I heard the scratching at the door. Bart Medlar was an alcoholic, deranged old coot. He had a still and made corn whiskey—from our corn, of course. His whiskey was wanted by everyone in the county and out of the county. He made some money now, but he didn't spend it on Mae or Johnny. C.W. did a lot of business with him years ago, didn't you, C.W.?"

C.W. nodded. "I took the whiskey to St. Louis and Chicago for the taverns and restaurants. Everyone wanted it. Bart had plenty of money. I have no idea what he did with it."

Violet calmly shared that last night with Mae.

"Violet, help me, please," Mae pleaded. "Bart's been out doing what he does with his homemade liquor from the still, and he's drunk. He came home to no food on the table. It's only because he doesn't give me money for food. He's beaten me for ten years, and I've allowed it."

"Mae had a laceration to the scalp as well as under her right eye. There were twelve cigarette burns on her arms, chest, and neck. Her face was so battered and swollen, it appeared distorted."

Mae was unsteady on her feet and confused. She insisted, "I want to leave Bart and never look back. Johnny is going to turn out just like him. Why kid myself? He already is."

"I cleaned every burn and treated each with antibiotic ointment. I sutured her head and her face. All the while I had ice on her face because of the swelling. One finger on her right hand was bent back and dislocated. I gave her a shot of whiskey and took one myself. It was heart wrenching to see another person treated so poorly. It was hard for me to deal with."

"I will probably die at Bart's hand," Mae told Violet.

"As I listened, I was massaging her hand and finger. Without warning, I pulled it hard to realign it. She was sobbing uncontrollably. Not from the pain, but from desperation," said Violet.

Violet offered, "Mae, I can take you to my sisters and let you live there and help her take care of her four children. Bart will never find you."

Violet let out a sigh. "I thought I had convinced her to leave."

"I can't take Johnny. He's already having mental issues. I wouldn't subject your sister to his behaviors. I can't leave him to face Bart alone," Mae said, sobbing.

"Mae, if you stay much longer, Bart will kill you."

"He's already killed. Two weeks ago, I think he killed Mary Robert's husband. Do you know her? Bob came to the house for whiskey and was arguing with Bart. I heard a gunshot, and I saw Bart with a shovel. I didn't dare ask questions."

"I know Mary," Violet said. "I will check on her this week. Haven't seen her in a while. You have to be safe, and you're not."

"Mae left anyway and went back to the shack. Bart killed her that very night. One of Bart's moonshine customers found her and called Sheriff Bone. Bart was passed out and had blood all over him.

"I went to see Mary the very next day," Violet shared. "Bob never came home after going for whiskey. Mary's house is falling down around her. Back porch is caved in, and she just sits on the front porch in the rocker every day waiting on him. I think Bart did kill him. I tried to get her to come here, and she wouldn't, so I just make sure she has food and visit her when I can.

"Bart's been in prison the past five years. No one knew where Johnny was when all of this went down.

"Johnny has had a devastating, abusive life. Bart put whiskey in his milk or water every day to shut him up. Bart despised a crying child and ridiculed him every day. It showed weakness. The child was tormented and punished every day of his existence. Then, when he got to crawling, Bart locked him in the pantry for days at a time. So, Johnny spent most of his day in a dark pantry closet, with no one. No food as we know it. Just darkness, and very little affection. He forbid Mary to let him out and took the keys with him. There was no heat in the house. This went on for ten years."

CHAPTER 7

"Let me tell you why Johnny hates us," Sam said. "Five years ago, when Bart went to prison, no one knew where Johnny was. Three days after Bart was taken to jail, I was coming home after dark. I had pulled off the highway at the crossroads and turned east on the dirt road to the farm. Snow was starting to stick, and snow fairies were bouncing off the windshield. I had put chains on the tires and was still sliding most of the way home. I was so worried about you, Sara, praying you weren't having a breathing issue due to the cold, damp weather and how it usually sets you into a wheezing episode.

"I checked the tree as I passed Pearline's house. There was no red rag flying, so I went on to our lane. I knew she was okay and didn't need to stop and check on her. At that moment, I saw movement at the mailbox, and I sat up straight, stretching my neck toward the windshield trying to see better through the snow. I thought I saw a child hanging on the mailbox, and I thought it had to be you, Sara. I was distraught at that point. The child had no clothes on. The child did not have red hair—it was black, and I saw Johnny clearly as I came to a stop next to the mailbox. I took my coat off as I exited the car and threw it around Johnny as I picked him up, sat him on the front seat, and turned the heat on high. He was skin and bones. You should have smelled him. It was disturbing.

"Johnny didn't utter a word. I carried him inside and sat him next to the stove on the rug. You were on the couch reading. Johnny kept staring at you. Violet brought hot soup in, and Jonny ate it like an animal. He hadn't had food for three days. I called Sheriff Bone to determine where he needed to go. I wasn't keeping him.

"While Violet and I were in the kitchen, Johnny lunged at you. I don't know why. You screamed at the top of your lungs. Johnny came at you again, and you did the old one-two kick into his balls to defend yourself. C.W. taught you that trick. I separated the two of you and didn't leave you alone with him anymore. I doubt you remember that night."

"Not really, Dad. It sounds awful. What a horrifying way to live," Sara responded.

"Sheriff Bone said one of Bart's whiskey customers couldn't find Bart, so he went in the house and heard Johnny screaming and cursing. He opened the pantry door with a screwdriver because it was locked. Johnny was at the bottom of the pantry under the shelf all cramped up. Johnny ran off in his filthy, stained underwear. That's how he ended up at our mailbox. Sheriff Bone took Johnny to the Boys' Ranch, and he was there until he turned eighteen, which was just a few days ago. His father was released from prison; therefore, Johnny was allowed to return to the farm."

"I went to the house with Sheriff Bone after Johnny was sent to the Boys' Ranch. The ranch catered to troubled and abandoned boys. The social workers called a dozen places to take Johnny. Not a single group home or residential care giver would accept him. He was too aggressive. I wanted to see if there was anything else that needed to be taken care of. I was really looking for Mr. Roberts, who had disappeared. The windows were cracked or broken. No heat was available. I think they spent most of their time outside by a fire. I saw the remnants of one. I looked in that pantry closet, and there was feces all over it. The odor was atrocious, and the claw marks on the inside of the door where Johnny tried to claw his way out filled me with such sadness, I hope I never experience it again.

"Johnny is a product of his environment, and we won't change him, nor can we help him. Too much damage is done. He needs professional help. Johnny wants to hurt us and will keep on trying. You cannot be alone anymore, and we all need to have a gun on us or one available. You see, Johnny had a rough time at the Boys' Ranch, but that will be discussed at a later time. He blames it on us, as we called the sheriff to take him away."

"Dad, that is devastating. I hurt for him, but I do know he wants to hurt me. What will happen to him? I need this to be over with. I'm either going to get my quiet, wholesome life back or lose the battle."

"There's no telling how this will end. Johnny is dangerous. We have to be very careful. Johnny is desperate now. He is focused on the farm and us. He wants to hurt us any way he can."

Sam was pacing back and forth across the room with obvious anxiety.

"I'm going to stay here for a while, Sara," C.W. said. "Something is going on mentally with Johnny. He is acting recklessly, almost desperate. I have seen this behavior before. I will be out in the fields and the woods on a daily basis and during the night. I will keep an eye on what he is doing."

Grandma was quiet. She didn't say a word, but she took a deep breath. Sam knew she was scared for Sara.

The following week, C.W. started teaching Sara gun safety. "Sara, I know you are aware I have guns all over this property." He smiled, remembering her jokes about the outhouse. "They are all loaded, so we need to talk about handling a gun safely. You may know a lot of this, but I want to go over it anyway."

"I'm ready, C.W. I've wanted to learn for a while now. It's not like I can go anywhere. I have to stay and see this through. I could end up dead or hurt."

"I won't let that happen. This is the beginning of learning to protect yourself. Let's get started."

They walked to the open chicken yard. C.W. stated, "Always keep the muzzle pointed away from yourself and in a safe direction. This means be aware of everyone and everything around you. Think about what you might hit in the distance if you fire. Never point your gun at anything you don't intend to shoot. We all know firearms should be unloaded when not in use. Unfortunately, with what is going on with Johnny, that rule is out of the picture and not up for discussion, as time is of the essence. A loaded gun with Johnny around will save your life.

"Never assume a gun is unloaded or loaded—check for yourself. Realistically, you should not cross a fence, climb, or crawl with a loaded gun. Never push or pull a loaded gun toward yourself or another person. Don't touch the trigger of a gun unless you aim to shoot it. Keep fingers away from the trigger, even if the safety is on. I have seen a gun fire after the safety is released. Always keep the safety on until you are ready to fire. Be aware of what your target is, and also what is behind your target. Don't fire at movement or noise without seeing what you are shooting at. You can kill someone by being reckless. Rifle bullets can travel over one and a quarter miles, shotgun pellets can travel over 500 yards, and a slug over half a mile. You have neighbors living in that range of fire. If your gun does not fire after the trigger is pulled, keep the muzzle in a safe position and unload the gun. Any questions on the basics? Does that make sense to you?"

"No questions. I understand what you are telling me," Sara replied.

"Now, let's talk about how to hold a handgun. For you, a two-handed grip is required. Hold the gun with your dominant hand on the back strap." C.W. demonstrated the grip with his gun. "Place

36

your non-dominate hand against the exposed portion of the grip. Your fingers on the support hand should be under the trigger guard, with your index finger pressed underneath." He pointed out every hand position and parts of the pistol. "Now, let me show you how to hold the gun. You are right-handed, so you grip with your right and the left hand curls around as a support."

Sara took the gun and positioned her right hand until she was comfortable. Then, she took her left hand and placed it under the trigger as a support. "Is this right, C.W.?"

"Yes, but Sara, you must secure it tighter.

"Now, I need you to stand with your feet shoulder width apart. Now, you have a firm foundation. Bend your knees. Use your dominant eye." C.W. moved behind Sara. "Hold the gun like you are ready to fire. Do you see the front and rear sight notch?"

C.W. curtly said, "Come on, Sara, hold the gun tight. You're going to get hurt if you don't."

"Yes, they are lined up," Sara confirmed. She felt his anger and felt hurt.

"C.W., I'm trying."

"I know you are. I'm worried about when I'm not here and Johnny, with his mental illness, comes around here to hurt you or Violet. I'm sorry. My fear is getting the best of me." C.W. hugged Sara, and she hugged him back. The more worried he was, the louder he got.

"I understand, C.W. I hope your lessons will prepare me for the worst."

C.W. instructed Sara, "First, align the top of the front sight with the top of the rear sight. You must look at three objects: front and rear sight and the target." C.W. set empty cans on a log for target practice. "Now, Sara, you show me."

Sara took her stance, put the pistol in her right hand, and wrapped the left hand securely. Sara aimed at the cans and looked down the sights. "I think I can do this part. It lines up well."

"Good job, Sara. Now, we need to load a magazine, which is difficult for some. Make sure you have the right ammunition. Check the label on the ammunition box. The caliber of your gun will be marked on the barrel of your gun." C.W. pointed to the markings on the muzzle and then showed her the label on the box. "Release the magazine by pressing the magazine release forward."

C.W. demonstrated by holding the magazine in his left hand. "Watch me use the ammo round to press down on the follower and slide the round under the feed lip. Use your support hand thumb to press down on rounds already in the magazine. Can you see how I am loading the ammo?"

"I know I will have to practice loading the magazine. My hands aren't as strong as yours. Let me practice it a while."

"No problem. Practice makes perfect. You will become an expert. You're a good student, Sara." He watched Sara work diligently at the task.

Grandma called out, "Lunch is ready."

When everyone was seated and the food passed, Sara remarked, "C.W. has been teaching me about gun safety and how to load a pistol. I'll be practicing on loading the magazine."

C.W. remarked, "Sara will do great with some practice. Tomorrow, we will shoot at targets. Let's put everything up for today. You can keep the magazine and ammo and work on getting faster at loading."

"I'll teach you how to shoot a rifle," Sam said. "You'll be able to shoot the eyes out of a snake as it is slithering away."

"Did you have to mention snakes, Dad?" Sara laughed. "Okay, that sounds like a plan."

Everyone had finished eating when Sam said he heard a horse coming up the lane. Sara jumped up and ran to the door. Willis was on his stallion, Wrangler. Sara ran out the door to greet him.

"Hi, Willis. What are you doing today?"

Willis smiled and held out a hand to pull her up behind him. "I came to take you for a ride."

Sara swung up behind Willis and commanded Sheba to stay.

Sam went to the door and waved as they galloped to the back of the property. C.W. joined him.

"Do you think Sara will be okay with a gun? Is she strong enough to shoot?" Sam asked C.W.

"I think with her determination, Sara can do anything. I promise I will teach her safety, and we will practice safely, too. Everything will be okay."

They could hear Sara squealing as they galloped away. Willis' dad and brothers came over at least once a month for Sunday dinner. It was always a fun time with laughing, jousting, and horse play. Baseball games were the best. Willis' mom had died years ago. Sam and Willis' dad, Mark, had grown up together. It didn't matter the time, if they needed help, they were there for each other. Willis had been Sara's best friend all of her life.

Sara looked at the light filtering through Lover's Lane. Birds were singing all around them. Shadows were filtered in the surrounding woods, with an occasional rabbit running for cover. As they cleared the lane, sunlight engulfed them. The woods flew by as they galloped on.

Willis pulled the reins in at the pond, and Wrangler drank water once they dismounted.

They were both growing up—him eighteen and her seventeen. She was no longer skinny, and her blue eyes put him into a trance. He liked her arms around him while they rode.

"I've been learning to shoot today," Sara told Willis. "It's so much fun. I have to practice loading the magazine. I'm not very good at that. I like it though."

"Wow. I didn't figure you to be interested in guns."

"Well, Johnny Medlar came back when his dad got out of prison. Unfortunately, they don't like us very well, and Johnny's been following me. We all thought it was time I had protection. Unfortunate, but it's a reality. Johnny scares me. I think he's crazy. I pray God will keep me safe and help me understand how he came to hate me. I don't want to hate him. I just want to protect myself. If I learn to shoot well, I hope I don't have to shoot him. That does worry me."

Will hugged Sara. "I hope that Johnny never touches you. I might have to step in and hurt him or shoot him myself."

"Don't say that. It would haunt us both for the rest of our lives."

"You're right. Let's walk around the pond, Sara. See any fish?"

"No, I don't fish, and I see snakes here. That means neither one is my favorite. Let's ride some more, Willis. I love riding with you. We don't do it enough."

"Okay, let's ride." He got the reins and mounted. Then, he pulled her behind him and felt her warmth on his back.

Willis and Sara were gone for several hours. Then, he dropped her off at the front door. Sara reached around and kissed him on the cheek before she dismounted. Willis smiled at her. He saw Sam at the garage and galloped over.

"Sounds like Sara is going to be a crack shot real soon."

"I can only pray I am doing the right thing. Old man Medlar and Johnny have me worried. Did you feel Sara was suffering related to Johnny? Did she talk about him?" Sam asked.

Willis shook his head. "She seems fine. I understand. If anything happens, just call, and Dad and I will be here to help."

"Thanks, Willis. Did you have fun riding?"

"We did. Sara loves riding through the woods. I better get home." Sam waved as he left.

Sara and C.W. were both up early the next day. Sara was excited about actually shooting at targets.

"Morning, sunshine. You ready to do some shooting?" C.W. asked Sara.

"I can hardly wait. Let's hurry up and eat."

Violet served the biscuits and gravy.

Violet asked C.W., "How long will you be able to stay?"

"At least another week. I have to spend some time outside after dark. I'm trying to establish a pattern on Johnny. I need to determine if he comes to our property every day, if he leaves his property, if he's bootlegging, or just what he is doing." There was no question about what had to be done. It was a matter of when and how.

"I'm sure that won't take you long," Sara said. "You have a lot of experience being aware of what's going on around you."

CHAPTER 8

"Sara, before dark today, I want you to walk through the field with me. I want both of us to just walk around his property. Not on it. We'll keep our distance. You have to know what his life is like. Understand?"

"Okay, C.W. I haven't paid any attention to that side of the property. I really don't go down there. I'd like to see it, though. None of this makes sense to me. The real problem is, I don't think anything makes sense to Johnny either. He's just a lost soul." Sara shrugged.

"Let's go shoot some targets, and then we'll head that way late afternoon. Grab your magazine."

"Okay, let me get it, and I'll meet you out there."

"Sara, I want you to put the magazine in the gun, and then you talk me through what you are doing."

Sara explained her actions. As she took aim, C.W. put his hand on her shoulder in support."

"Squeeze ever so gently, but firmly. Keep your eye on the target."

She missed the first target.

"Again, Sara. This is all about practice."

Practice continued for several hours, and she began hitting more frequently.

"Great job, Sara. I need to help your dad a while. Then, we'll walk down by the Medlar place. See you in a while."

Sara continued to practice. She failed to notice C.W.'s approach later, being deep in thought and intent on hitting the target.

"It's time to go, Sara. Put your boots on. We're walking in high grass and in wooded areas. We need two hours to walk the outer boundaries of the property, and I will probably see things I want to question more."

They crossed behind the garden and entered the cornfield. They headed southeast and stood hidden in the depths of the cornfield overlooking the gravel road in front of Medlar's property. "Starting today, you need to be observant of everything. The woods are dense. Therefore, you have to look beyond the leaves. Listen for animals scurrying off or birds taking flight. It often means something or someone has scared them."

All they saw was a green inferno that had smothered all the trees, the wooden fence, and even a portion of the house. The creeping vines went over the land like a border wall covering everything. The mounds of green covered the yard, the banks, and anything lying on the ground.

"This is eerie, C.W. How do you know where to go in, and what is under all of these leaves?"

"You don't know. This is kudzu. It has spread and enveloped the whole property because no one was here for years. I see a short dirt road turning into the property, but the road is solid kudzu. It has devoured everything. It hogs the sunlight, so everything dies beneath it. I bet there is no grass surrounding the house. It's like a fast-growing cancer that is difficult to get rid of.

"Let's keep walking. I'm interested in what is around the house and barn that used to be here. The still used to be on the east side of the house. The barn was 100 feet to the south of the house. Kudzu has tangled, woody branches close to the ground and vines that can travel over 100 feet. You can get tangled up in this mess."

They both heard a car engine come to life, and they dove to the ground, keeping their heads low. C.W. was watching the short road that disappeared into the kudzu.

Johnny slid through the kudzu where the road ended. He started pulling and straining as the muscles on his arms and shoulders were defined. Then, the kudzu started to rise as he pulled the gate toward him. The gate was covered solid with vines—a work of ingenuity to hide from the world. As he pulled taut on the rope with the pulley attached, the wall and gate of green rose. Johnny secured the rope by securing it on the pole. Then, he strode back to the car, slammed the door, and drove through.

The car stopped again. Johnny stepped out of the car, unwrapped the rope, and lowered the gate. He was limping. He stepped back to see if everything was covered and secure. Johnny looked down the road and into the cornfield as though he could see Sara and C.W., who were frozen in place hugging the ground. Then, he and the old black Ford were gone.

Sara and C.W. slid down the bank of their property and crossed through the cattails and milk weeds to the gate. "I know I said we wouldn't go on the property, but this is an opportunity I didn't foresee," C.W. said in a whisper.

"Sara, don't walk in the dusty lane. The footprints will show. He'll know someone was here. Walk on the edge of the kudzu. It's uneven, so don't turn your ankle."

They edged up the drive and saw the kudzu thinned out around three sides of the house. There was a trail in five directions. It was obvious someone had been clearing the kudzu from the property. A machete lay on the ground beside the water pump. Most of the ground was dirt and dusty. The fence lines were covered with Morning Glory flowers. Birds were in flight above them, and squirrels jumped from branch to branch. Rabbits ran for the kudzu.

"I think they need some goats," Sara said. She looked at the vine next to her, which was long and hairy. The leaves were huge. She tried to separate and see inside the wall of green, but the formation was thick and hard to pull or get into. It was as though it were able to strangle everything in its path. "Let's see where the paths go to," Sara said, pointing.

"Stay close to me and listen for movement of anything," C.W. said firmly. "Old man Medlar may be around, or he may be drunk. He loves his whiskey."

They walked on. The first path came out in the field that was in front of Pearline's house. The second went to the barn. The weathered barn sat at an angle, as though leaning into the wind. The other three paths went to the far corners of Sam's property. Johnny was keeping an eye on everyone's routine on Sam's property. As they came around the east side of the house, the ground was bare and the still was getting repaired to be back in business. Tools were lying beside it. The still had been taken apart, and it looked like someone was cleaning the pipes.

Sara spotted Bart Medlar first. Out cold on the front porch. They lived in squalor. C.W. took Sara's hand and pulled her toward the road they'd entered on. They avoided the old truck and washing tub at the edge of the kudzu.

"Let's get out of here, NOW," C.W. said with urgency.

Sara stopped. "I hear a car. Run." She and C.W. started for the gate, but he pulled her to him.

"We won't make it. There's no way to cross the road to our property without being seen. We have to go into the kudzu at a weak spot. You have to be quiet. Don't let go of me. We will go through the gate as soon as we can. We can get through at the edge of it. I already checked."

"Okay. I'm with you."

They backtracked twenty feet. Then, they both disappeared into a green blanket of coverage and darkness. They stood silent in the kudzu. Johnny turned in the driveway and released the gate. He then drove right by them. Sara's nose was itching, and she wanted to sneeze. As the car disappeared, C.W. pulled Sara to the gate and pushed her through the narrow opening, following on her heels. They ran for the ditch and crawled up the bank, disappearing into Sam's cornfield.

"I don't ever want to do that again," Sara exclaimed. She was pulling at leaves stuck in her hair. Her nose was running, and she was sneezing.

C.W. looked at Sara. He stopped her and took her face in his hands. "Don't you ever go there without me. Do you understand?"

"Yes, I understand." Sara sneezed six more times and smiled at C.W. "Allergic to the kudzu. I don't want to go there ever again if I don't have to. I am scared of Johnny and his dad. I know the history of the property and the people who live there is hidden under the kudzu. It's just a matter of time before someone digs up the truth."

Little did Sara know how true that statement would turn out to be.

C.W. went to find Sam. "Sara and I walked around Medlar's property," he said. "There are five trails cut out, and three come to your farm. The boy is watching all the time. Sara needed to see what surrounds the farm. This is a dangerous situation when you're dealing with an alcoholic and a kid with mental illness. Don't leave Sara by herself. You know I have to head back to Chicago in a few days."

"I know the worst is yet to come," Sam replied.

CHAPTER 9

Sam left late the next day to get farm supplies. "Violet, keep an eye on Sara. Make sure she has access to a gun if you are out in the garden or anything."

"I will, Sam. I'm just as worried as you. I have to check Christine today. I told Doc I would help him. He'll be by in an hour to pick me up. I'll let Sara know and tell her not to leave the house."

Two hours after Violet left, Sara saw an old grey sedan pull in the driveway. The driver was driving like a bat out of hell. A large man in work pants and a shirt jumped from the vehicle and bounded up the steps. He was banging on the door yelling, "Violet," as Sara opened it. Sara recognized him as Tim Martin. He had been to the farm before to see Sam.

"I need Violet now. My boy's hurt bad and bleeding from a knife wound."

"She won't be back for two hours. She's with Dr. Gerstein at Christine Mark's place. I know how to suture, if that's what you need. Grandma taught me, and I help her sometimes. I've probably done two dozen wound sutures."

Tim ran his fingers through his hair and shifted his weight from foot to foot, considering. "Okay, let's go," he said.

Sara wrote a quick note saying where she was and why. "Get what you need," Tim demanded.

Sara told Sheba, "Stay." Sheba whined in response. Sara looked for the medical bag, some bandages, and disinfectant and then ran for the car. The ride was less than enjoyable as they careened down the country road.

They entered the house, and she saw several men standing around. They were all packing guns. Sara was observant as she entered. The young man was on his back on the kitchen table. He was barely conscious. He was pale, diaphoretic, with shallow breathing. Blood was spreading over his white shirt as though the tide were carrying the blood into shore.

She pulled a tourniquet from the bag and secured it above the wound in his arm. Sara pulled out the hemostats after donning gloves and began to probe. The three-inch wound was gaping, and bone was visible. The bleeder was spurting, and she clamped the artery quickly. Sara was preparing to suture the wound closed when the front screen door banged against the wall. She jumped. Johnny moved in close behind Sara to where she could feel his warmth and breath.

"I've been looking for you, girl," Johnny whispered.

Sara picked up the scalpel and whirled on him. Johnny jumped away. Sara looked at Tim. "If you want me to save your son, get him out of this house. I have no time for this, and neither does your son." Sara pointed at Johnny. In one step, Tim grabbed Johnny by the shirt collar, kicked open the screen door, and shoved Johnny hard. Johnny cleared the steps and landed face first. They saw the hate emanating from him. Tim stood in the doorframe with a planted, wide stance, his right hand on the butt of his holstered gun. He glared at Johnny. "I can see you have something going for her, but I want you to know after someone helps me, I'm loyal. If

48

you ever touch her, I'll kill you. Do you hear?" Tim folded his arms in a gesture of finality.

Johnny looked from one man to the next and then sneered. He walked away, nodding his head.

"Thank you," Sara said. "He's been trouble for me the last few weeks. Do you have a phone? I'll call Dr. Gerstein to come and see your son."

Tim nodded.

Sara finished suturing and put a pressure bandage on the wound. Tim nodded toward the phone on the counter. Sara called Christine's house. The phone rang.

"This is Sara. Is Violet and Doc still there?"

"Yes, I'll get Doc."

Sara explained what was going on. "Can you stop and leave pain medication and something for infection? I think he needs intravenous fluids. He lost a lot of blood." Mainly, she really wanted Doc to check her work.

"Of course, Sara. Are you okay? Tell Tim I'll be there in thirty minutes."

"Tim's going to take me home now. I'm good. I just want to make sure I did everything I needed to for his son."

It was well after dark when they rolled into the driveway of the farm. Sam rushed out the door of the house and asked Sara, "Are you all right?" Sara could see C.W. in the shadows.

"I am, Dad. I had to suture his son. He was bleeding bad from a knife wound. Grandma was gone." Sam knew Tim well, and they shook hands as Tim exited the car.

"We had a little run-in with the Medlar boy. He delivered whiskey to the house and saw Sara there. I put him in his place," Tim remarked.

Sara softly said, "Johnny hates me."

Knowing what he did about Johnny, Sam faced the reality that Sara might not be too far from the truth. They said their goodbyes, and Sara and Sam turned to go inside. Tim reached out to Sam and handed him several hundred dollars. "It's for Sara when she needs something. I'll always be indebted to her for saving my son." Tim took a deep breath. "I'd better get back to my son. Doc is coming."

Sam, C.W., and Sara were at the table eating tomato sandwiches when Violet returned with Doc.

"Sara, you did a fine job suturing that boy."

"Thanks. I did my best. With all the knowledge Grandma has given me, I've decided I'm going to nursing school as soon as I can."

"That is awesome, Sara. We are all so proud of you."

Sam laughed. "That's good Sara because Tim gave me $300 for you, and it can go towards college."

"Dad, you know C.W. already promised to pay for my college. Maybe I'll buy some new shoes. I need some high heels." They all laughed. In reality, as Sam and C.W. looked at Sara, they could see she was blossoming into a young woman. That just brought more problems.

CHAPTER 10

The following day, Sara took Sheba and decided to walk the property. It was a beautiful morning, with a soft wind sweeping over the treetops. The clouds were feathered with the colors of pink and white pearls. Sara knew that was her blessing for the day.

A red fox looked at them and trotted off. Sheba paid it very little attention but was aware of its presence.

Sara relaxed as she went through lover's lane headed for the cemetery. The sunlight filtered through the trees in minute spots. The lane was always cool and shadowed. She had picked roses for her mother's grave.

"Sheba, you are such a good girl. I love having you with me. Fact is, I don't know what I would do without you. I just wish you could talk to me. You would have a lot to say. I just know it." Sara reached down and patted Sheba's back as she and Sheba knelt in front the grave. Sara looked at the ground in the middle of the cemetery headstones. Something looked odd. As she stepped on the upraised ground, it sounded hollow. Sheba stepped in front of her to stop her from going farther. "I'll have to remember to tell Dad about this," Sara murmured, and walked on with Sheba by her side.

Sara was curious about the Medlar boy, but cautious knowing what he was capable of. They walked around the edge of the cornfield where she could see the Medlar property. They sat in the shade of the old oak watching and listening. Sheba picked up on the sound first and cocked her head toward the cry. "What was that noise, Sheba? Probably a cat." Later, Sara could hear arguing, but she couldn't make out the words. She knew it was a man and a woman. Occasionally, Sara heard a cracking noise and then a moan. Sarah was leery of the unknown and stood. Sheba started nudging her to go back towards the house, but Sara walked closer to the Medlar's property. Sheba gave a low growl, blocking her progress. Sara stopped. She had promised C.W. to never go on the property by herself. She turned around and headed for the house.

The newspaper lay open on the table with the headlines exposed: *LOCAL GIRL MISSING*. Sara drew the paper to her and read the story. She flung the newspaper down and stalked to her room. Sheba lay on the floor and watched her closely. She could smell the fear on Sara. Sara's mind was in turmoil with questions. *How sick is Johnny? Could he be hurting someone at his property? Could he kill someone?* Sheba crept up onto the foot of the bed and laid her head on Sara. Sara hugged her tight.

At dinner that evening, Sara was oddly quiet and only answered questions from her Grandma and Dad. "Dad, next time you go to the cemetery, look in the middle of the graveyard. Something is odd with the ground. A grave sounded hollow when I stepped on it."

Sam and Violet looked at each other. She just didn't want to talk about what she had heard at Medlar's place and didn't trust her instincts. Maybe she was letting her imagination get the best of her. She didn't eat much and went to her room. Sara tried to read to distract herself from her own thoughts. The vivid memories of Johnny left her distraught. When Sam checked on her as he was going to bed, she had fallen asleep.

Sara awoke with a start. The night was silent except for the locusts. The sheer drapes were ever so lightly dancing in the fleeting breeze. Sara raised up on her elbows and peered out the window, watching for anything to move. A chill went up her spine when she heard the terrified scream in the distance. Sara bolted out of bed and dressed quietly. She went to her father's room. He was snoring lightly. "Dad, Dad. You have to get up. Someone's in trouble."

"What? Who's in trouble? Are you okay, Sara?"

"Yes, yes. It's not me, Dad. I need you to come and listen to something outside. She pulled him to the window in her room. "Sit down and listen." Then, a high-pitched scream of agony and terror was heard in the distance. Sam and Sara looked at each other.

"I have to get dressed," Sam said. "Do you know something more about this?"

Sara relayed her experience with Sheba earlier in the day. "I should have gone with my instinct. I just don't want you to think I'm going nuts after all that's happened with Johnny. I know something bad is happening at the Medlar house. Let's go to the edge of the cornfield and determine if it's coming from there, and then we can call for help."

Sara put on her boots and hoodie as she waited for Sam to get ready. Sam came to her door with a rifle and a pistol on his hip. She took her pistol and secured her gun belt.

"Sara, I think C.W. is rubbing off on us. Just for the record, I don't think you're nuts. We are all stressed out after dealing with Johnny."

Sam and Sara went to the back of the house and crossed through the garden to the cornfield. The moonlight lit their path, but the shadows made them uneasy. Both were scanning the property as they walked. When they reached the gravel road, they crouched down and listened. Then, the high-pitched scream came again. Sara clamped her teeth together and felt a chill crawl over her. Sam just put his hand on her arm and a finger to his lips. They heard a male voice threaten, "I'm going to beat you til you bleed." Then, a female voice said, "Please don't hurt me anymore. I haven't done anything." The sobbing continued.

"We need to go back to the house and call Sheriff Bone," Sam remarked. "He has the authority to go on the property. There's something real bad going on here, and we can't just go over there and get in a gun fight."

"Okay, but I'm coming with you when he gets here. I know the lay of the land and where the buildings are. You're not going to talk me out of it either," Sara told her dad. They practically ran to the house.

Sam called the sheriff and gave him a brief rundown. "No sirens, Sheriff. We may want to walk in, so he can't escape. I don't know if it's Johnny or Bart."

Both went outside to wait. Thirty minutes later, they were in front of Medlar's property with the sheriff, a deputy, and Sheba. They cautiously crossed the gravel road and slipped between the gate and tree onto Medlar's property. They stayed on the dirt road close to the kudzu wall.

The darkness was intense. There was a lone light in the distance beckoning them on. They reached the dilapidated barn and peered through the cracks in the wall. At first, they didn't see anyone. Then, they heard a moan farther into the barn. Quietly, they edged their way around to the opposite side. Sara motioned everyone to get down low as the opening revealed a girl and Johnny. The girl was cornered and trying to run for the door. Her face was swollen, and her lips were bleeding.

Johnny took his belt in hand and laid a scarlet stripe across her breast first, then her thigh. Sara felt sick from such cruelty and could feel her heart racing. The girl kicked Johnny with such force, he went down on one knee to the wooden floor. Johnny was outraged now and went into a frenzy. He ripped the remainder of her shirt from her and lashed at her with the belt. The metal buckle caught her shoulder, and she screamed in agony. Johnny's face held a smile of enjoyment and contempt. He glimpsed her white thigh, and the belt sliced into her flesh. Johnny was aroused by her fear.

Sheriff Bone and the deputy were heading for the doors of the barn. The next minute was complete chaos. The girl hit Johnny in the head with a loose horseshoe. She used every bit of strength she had left knowing she would die here. Johnny fell with such force his face hit the dirt and scraped the plow as he went down. The sheriff and deputy had guns drawn as the doors burst open. The girl was lucky she wasn't shot, as the sheriff hadn't expected anyone to be running to them. The girl didn't stop. She was crazed and ran like a hunted animal. "I'm going to make it," she kept repeating. She thought she heard someone chasing and turned to look. She fell.

Sara was already on the move when the girl swung the horseshoe. She took her jacket off as she ran and was right behind the girl as she bolted from the garage. "You're safe. We're with the sheriff."

The girl looked dazed but allowed Sara to put her jacket around her. Her violent sobbing was heart-wrenching.

As Johnny stumbled out of the barn, he let out an anguished roar that scared the girl enough to get up and try to run again. Sheba was in front of Johnny, growling. He stopped. Sara put her arms around the girl as the sheriff approached Johnny, threw him to the ground, and cuffed him.

The deputy went for the car and pulled up to the property. He offered water to the girl. Her lips were cracked and bleeding, but she drank.

Johnny looked at Sara. As Sara was walking to the road to go home, Johnny turned to her. "Your day is coming," he said.

Sara kept walking and didn't acknowledge him.

The girl was the missing girl from the newspaper bulletin. Her name was Marilyn Sheets. She had been flirting with Johnny at the store, and he offered to take them to get something to eat. That was two days ago. Marilyn was taken to the hospital as a rape victim—but turns out she hadn't been raped. She confessed that she'd gone to the house willingly—but not knowing the conditions she was walking into. Johnny testified that she liked the pain and asked him to hurt her. Stated it was a cat and mouse game, and she liked it when they first got to the barn. He was charged with a misdemeanor and sixty days in jail.

The Boys' Ranch in which Johnny had been was abusive in so many ways. He was often forced to stay outside in a fenced area for punishment, whether there was rain, thunder, or lightning. He had his head slammed against the wall daily for any infraction. He was sexually abused by the other boys for years. His bipolar disorder with dissociation was presenting. He was abused at home every day of his life. The information was good to know but really insignificant when you looked at the whole picture. It was too late—too late to help him, too late to save him, and most of all, too burdensome to worry and wonder who his next victim would be.

CHAPTER 11

The days were peaceful at the farm. Fall had arrived, and the breeze made you wrap up in a sweater and enjoy the essence of the calm day. Winter was right around the corner. Today, they were all safe. The garden had flourished, and Violet and Sara were pulling up the remnants of the harvest. The foliage was maroon and gold. Two large pumpkins sat on the porch. The cushions in the rockers were changed to orange. Everything said fall was here.

"Sara, are you okay?" her grandma asked. "It's been a bad year with Johnny returning to the area. I find myself worrying more, but today is a calmer day within myself knowing Johnny is behind bars."

"Grandma, none of this seems real to me. I bet no one I know has ever dealt with this shit. You couldn't even make this up. Johnny has done one favor for me. I am always aware of my surroundings, and it will be good for me when I go to Chicago to school in a few months. It will keep me on my toes, and it will be hard for me to trust anyone."

"I understand that. You wearing that shoulder holster every day when you leave the house reminds me of C.W. I can't wait for you to get your nursing license. I will live the rest of my life through yours. Hopefully, you will be close by when you get a job, and I will tag along." Her grandma laughed.

"I really plan to come back here and take care of the people in this county. I'll work part-time at the hospital, but I want to grow and be productive all my life. Basically, I am like you. I want to serve others while I serve my God," Sara shared. "Does that make sense?"

Grandma replied, "It surely does make sense. I'm so proud of you, Sara."

"Thanks, Grandma. I love you."

Sam stopped by the sheriff's office before heading home. "Sherriff Bone, how are you this fine day?" Sam asked.

"Nothing quite as exciting as the time I spend at your place." They both chuckled. "Johnny is behind bars but will be out before Christmas. I will definitely call and give you the day he will be released. There is something seriously wrong with that kid. You know that, don't you, Sam?"

"Yes, I'm aware. I believe he will continue this erratic behavior until someone kills him. I just hope it's not one of my family that has to pull the trigger. Sara learned how to shoot earlier in the year, and she's pretty darn good, if I do say so myself. I pray it's not her, but I think she has had enough. He could overpower her easily. This kid is going to have to go one way or another," Sam commented.

"He's dangerous," Sheriff Bone stated, without blinking an eye. "He does some crazy things here. Always talks to himself. Almost like he sees someone in the cell with him. My boys always walk away shaking their heads. When the social worker spoke with him, he told her no one would ever care how he felt, and no one would help him. He had no one. No one at all. Said he was good-for-nothing like his dad told him every day. Not one person cared. He was all alone."

What happened next seemed like a turning point in Sara's life. Willis came up from the east side of the house on Wrangler. He was initially hidden from the farmhouse. Sara saw him first and ran outside.

"Why are you riding in from the woods?"

"I just wanted to ride by Medlar's place and take a look. Let's ride, Sara," said Willis.

As they rode off to the stream, Willis paused under the old oaks and dismounted Wrangler. He took the rolled blanket off the back of the saddle and spread it out. With Sara's hand in his, he guided her to the blanket. Willis leaned against the bole of the tree and pulled Sara close. The woodland and fields stretched out in front of them. The dried, golden grass swayed slightly. Two fences were leaning with age. It was so familiar to Sara that she did not linger on the view. Willis looked down at Sara.

"You're the prettiest girl I have ever seen." Her lips were pink, soft, and moist. Her red and gold hair framed her flawless face. Her waist was tiny. Sara saw his eyes and enjoyed the moment. She lifted a hand to his chest and lay her head there, snuggling closer. She raised her mouth and gently kissed him. The silence was broken only by Willis' breathing. He felt strangely moved by the contact of Sara's warmth and felt weak.

"Are you all right?" Sara asked.

"I've never been better," Willis replied with a grin. He placed an arm around her shoulder. "I love spending time with you. You are my first and only true love, Sara."

"You mean everything to me as well, Willis," Sara replied, giving him an adoring smile and wriggling closer. Later, Sara rose and stepped into the creek. Willis removed his boots.

He looked at her dainty feet, as they relished the cool water on their legs. Willis stooped to kiss Sara, searching for her mouth. Sara was the first to pull back. Her breath was warm on his neck and tickled. He felt her tongue flitter across his lips. It excited him in a way he knew nothing of.

The sun was high over the trees when they remounted Wrangler. They rode over the road a piece and then went around the cattle grid that stopped anyone from getting to Grandma's home. It was set deep in the woods and surrounded by cornfields. They walked through the gate and followed the stone path surrounding the house. The flowers were in full bloom.

"This house is so peaceful within the shadows. I feel at home here," Willis commented.

Sara smiled. "I know. I love it here, too."

They roused themselves from the contentment and rode home. Willis watched Sara disappear into the house and grinned as he galloped home. He knew he had an honest, pure love for Sara, and it filled his very soul.

CHAPTER 12

It was a Saturday morning in Chicago. A bright and sunny cool day for a walk. C.W. had his bodyguards, and they were looking for information. They wanted the name of the boss who had ordered those goons to his establishment, which resulted in the death of his men. C.W. had been more selective on the jobs he did lately. He was known to do a hit or two and even a favor for the right amount of cash.

C.W. thought about what he had done in his lifetime. He wasn't wanting to feel any regret, but his thoughts always went to Sara. What would she think of him when he was gone? There were poker games coming up, with huge investors. It was important there be no gun play. Under the table payoffs for illegal gambling in his establishment was a hefty amount. C.W. still hooked up with the St. Louis racketeers when the need arose. He was doing more in the arena of labor racketeering, horse racing, real estate development, and loan companies.

It was a non-productive day. Every door they knocked on, the lieutenants were out. So, they wandered around.

Sullivan brought C.W. back to the events at hand. "So, no one's talking. They've got no reason to lie to us. I find that hard to believe. Let's get a drink."

They entered the closest pub on the east side. They were all on high alert to their surroundings and finished their beers in silence. Sullivan worked the clientele. Just a little small talk and leading questions didn't get them anywhere. Under dark of night, they headed to the upper east side where the Chicago Outfit could be found. They only needed one man to pressure into spilling his guts about the intrusion. They looked for a contact who would fold quickly. Younger and no experience was good.

They found that unlucky mafia soldier on Michigan Street. They walked briskly through the high-end residential area. Very few pedestrians were out. Sullivan spotted the nonchalant mafia soldier outside the red brick home. C.W.'s driver pulled up to the soldier and rolled down the window, posing to ask a question. At the same time, C.W. and Sullivan threw him in the back of the sedan and disarmed him. They gunned the sedan and headed for the shore of Lake Michigan. C.W. started the interrogation.

"You have anything to say about what went down at Sara's Club several weeks ago?"

Not a word came from him. A plane roared above them, like thunder rolling in a bad storm. Then, the soldier spoke. His eyes narrowed and his nerves got the best of him. His voice was low. "You stepped into the Outfitter's territory. Taking too much business and losing money. The boys are in the house deciding what to do about you. The boss is in there, too."

Twelve minutes later, they knew who, what, when, and where the boss was. They tossed the soldier in Lake Michigan, then returned to the brick house where they had started.

"Boss, what do you want us to do with the guys inside? They're not going to take this lying down," Sullivan stated.

"They're just neighborhood gangsters. What's troubling you? We kill them just like they did McCoy and Morgan."

When the gunfire was over, they strode through the house looking for loot. "Look, boss. The strongbox is full of silver and gold.
Probably, it was the payload from one of their heists."

"It's all good. Now, it's Sara's."

Seven men died that night, and C.W. was two million richer.

Sullivan was satisfied with his cut. C.W. was good to him.
"Thanks, boss. I'm saving up for a rainy day just like you. We may
get out of this business alive, yet."

The sixty days jail time went all too swiftly. Sara's world stopped
the day Sheriff Bone came to the farm.

"Unfortunately, Johnny will be released Saturday," Sheriff Bone
announced. "We both know a restraining order won't do a thing.
He will do whatever he wants. Johnny is bona fide crazy," said
Sheriff Bone.

Sam put his arm around Sara. "We'll be careful." He turned to
Sara. "It's important you stay close to the house, have Sheba with
you all the time, and you have to be packing every time you are
outside."

"I know, Dad. I'll do what you say." Sara looked at Sheriff Bone.
"Wish us luck. We're going to need it."

Sara went inside. She didn't tell her dad or grandma, but she
called C.W. Sullivan answered at the bar.

"Sullivan, this is Sara. I need to talk to C.W. immediately."

In seconds, C.W. answered. "What's wrong, Sara?"

"Johnny's out of jail in three days. I have a bad feeling. I think
he is sicker than ever. Sheriff Bone says he is chanting in his cell and
talks to someone in the cell who isn't there. I'm afraid I will have to
kill him, C.W. Can you come home?"

C.W.'s heart broke. "HOME." Sara didn't know how that word,
the farm, was what he thought of as home. He knew she was scared.
"I'll be there in two days. I have some unfinished business. My

gambling ventures have to go even further underground. Even a new location. All the big money is in gambling. One gang trying to oust another. The new bosses on the north side are thinking bigger and more dangerous than ever before. Two days is all I need."

He and the boys were planning on breaking into the biggest warehouse in downtown Chicago—a stone monster that covered a whole block. It had confiscated liquor, guns, and valuables from heists gone bad. C.W.'s boy, Slim, was on the inside on their payroll double dipping. C.W. knew how everything was to go down.

C.W. and ten of his boys were hidden, watching every move. The sedan rolled by, and in seconds, five men and their boss jumped out and hugged the warehouse shadows. One knocked on the wooden door. The inside warehouse guard cracked the door, peered out, and was down for the count. He took one punch to the jaw. The doors were opening for the five-ton truck careening around the building. It stopped with a screech, backed up, and plowed into the warehouse. The boys jumped out of the truck and loaded the booze and guns.

When the last case was loaded, all hell broke loose. Robbers robbing robbers. Guns were blazing. C.W. and his boys moved in and started firing, taking down Outfitter's boss and ten pals. Four of C.W.'s boys jumped into the truck and drove it to the docks. The warehouse at the dock was a new location to take the heat off the pub. The boys unloaded the truck and drove it into Lake Michigan. Time to lay low for a while. C.W. called the boys together.

"Sullivan, you take the boys back to the bar. I don't want the events of tonight discussed with anyone. Don't talk about it to each other. You never know who is listening or who works for the Outfitters. The police will be out in full force, and some are on their payroll. Stay away from the warehouse. Be on high alert at the bar and wherever you go. They will want to know who has their goods and killed their boys. Any questions? I'll be out of pocket for a while," C.W. announced.

64

C.W. had been right. The media was all over the story, and they were looking for who had carried out the heist. The bodies reflected one gang and bloodshed. Nervous police were guarding banks and patrolling streets everywhere. They were looking for C.W. and several other mobsters for questioning. When the police questioned Sullivan and the boys, they still didn't have a clue as to who had hit the warehouse.

CHAPTER 13

There was a sliver of moon over the farm when C.W. rolled in. He went to Violet's old farmhouse to avoid waking anyone. The cattle guard rumbled as he crossed. He parked the car and immediately walked to the Medlar property. C.W. could smell booze in the wings of the breeze that carried him straight to Medlar's still. He stood behind the tree and watched a slow grin crease Bart Medlar's craggy face.

C.W. thought, *God only knows what he's thinking of tonight.* The still had been totally repaired since his last visit to Medlar's place. It was cranking. Like a shadow, he left the property and headed back to the house.

He had one more thing to do before Johnny got out, and tonight was the only night he had. Otherwise, he would have to watch his every move, and Johnny might be watching him. He had brought the trunk of silver and gold coins with him. It was for a rainy day. He took canning jars from Violet's shed and placed them on the kitchen table. He then filled each one. C.W. went to the henhouse, which no longer had chickens, and dug a hole in the left corner. He secured the jars in the hole, covered them with dirt, and spread the straw. Anyone entering the henhouse would never know anything had been disturbed. He then did the same at the outhouse. That was just a bad decision. C.W. snickered as he thought about Sara's response to his choice of treasure location. The doghouse was the last area. The ground didn't look like it had ever been disturbed.

After the job was complete, he wrote a message just like a treasure map for Sara to have if anything should happen to him. Violet would keep it for Sara, until the time was right. She would be taken care of. He knew she had saved everything he had ever given her. She already had millions, but you'd never know it. He placed the answers in another envelope for Violet to give to Sara if she didn't succeed on the scavenger hunt. He knew Sara would laugh and say, game on.

You laughed about my habits once and where my three treasures are.
1. You feed me, you take from me, and you enjoy me.
2. You use me, it wasn't pleasing to you, but it's necessary.
3. Your most treasured possession lies in it.

The next morning, C.W. waited by the corn crib for Sam. C.W. stepped from the shadows.

"Don't do that, C.W. We're all touchy. It's a good way to get killed," Sam said, but he was excited to see him. "Do you have troubles in Chicago?"

"Maybe a little. We heisted a warehouse from Outfitters and left a few dead. Wasn't a lot of information yet about the investigation. Probably will be by tonight. Let's see how accurate it is."

Sam just shook his head.

"Want some advice, brother?" Sam asked. "Get out while you can. Alive and in one piece. You're getting older."

"I know. I know. I don't know if I can get out or how to get out anymore. I hate leaving the boys to take the heat. Don't like the idea of getting caught either. They would have a hell of a time proving anything was connected to me. I'd love to maybe buy a spread like yours." Then, the conversation was brought up about Johnny being released. "What's your take on Johnny?" C.W. didn't mention Sara calling him, and Sam was none the smarter about their conversation and her fearing for her life. C.W. was ready.

"We have to keep Sara safe. Johnny is going to hurt her first chance he gets." Sam looked at C.W. and sighed. "We will probably kill Johnny real soon. It's inevitable, with his state of mind. I will not allow him to hurt anyone else. It has gone too far."

"Sam, let me take care of it. Don't dirty your hands. He will be on your property, and we will finish the deed."

CHAPTER 14

Pearline was up early that Saturday morning, just like every day of her life. She unlocked the front door and called "Kitty, kitty, kitty." The cats didn't come, and she started to step outside. Directly in front of the door was what appeared to be blood. Pearline saw movement and tried to step back into the house. She wasn't fast enough. Johnny had her pinned against the door frame, glaring at her. Fear filled Pearline like water being poured into a vessel. Little did she know something had snapped in his mind.

Johnny started pushing her into the house as he slammed the door behind him. She felt the whole house shake. Pearline turned to protect herself but was too late. She lost her balance and fell to the floor. Johnny was on her with a full armlock to the neck. He was blocking her windpipe. She couldn't breathe. He released her in just a few seconds. Pearline's mouth was wide open, gasping for air. She waited silently for what was coming. She could hear her own labored breathing. The wheezing air was rushing in and out of her lungs.

With a stone-cold face, Johnny looked at her. "I need money. Where do you have your money?" Johnny was consumed with rage. Pearline waited for opportunity, but she was almost eighty and weak. She knew she couldn't run. Thoughts ran through her mind. *Today may be my last day on this earth.*

"I live on social security. I maybe only have twenty dollars in this house. Now, get out."

Johnny took her wrist and twisted. Pearline felt her wrist snap and gave a cry. She paled from the pain.

"Where is the twenty dollars? Get it, NOW."

Pearline stumbled to the cabinet and took the money from behind the canned peaches.

He grabbed the money from her and stormed to the door. He turned and looked at Pearline. "Tell that girl that comes to see you, I'm watching, and she's next."

Pearline recoiled in astonishment. The dread and fear of the intent of his words consumed her. The adrenaline was gone now, and she was weak and shaking. She was able to slide down the wall, supporting her arm the last foot before she was on the floor.

It was some time before Pearline recovered. Her wrist was swollen and painful. Pearline tried to push herself up from the floor but fell back. With a clearer head now, the realization of Sara's danger was sharp and stark. It drove her on. She had to get to the phone. Desperately, Pauline pushed herself across the floor to the far wall and drew closer to the phone. Fear for Sara kept her moving inch by inch. She got her legs under her and pushed herself to her knees. Finally, she pulled the phone from the cradle and called Sara's house. Sam answered as he and Violet were the early risers.

"Hello?"

"Sam, it's Pearline. I need help," she whispered.

"What's wrong?" Sam didn't wait for an answer. He grabbed his keys to the car. "Violet, come on. Pearline's in trouble."

Violet turned the stove off and dropped her apron, which was dusted with flour. The bread baking would just have to wait. Violet grabbed her sweater as she followed Sam to the door.

"What did she say?"

"Just that she needed help."

In just a few minutes, they pulled into her circle drive and jumped out. Sam had his pistol drawn, not knowing what he was walking into. They entered the front door and saw Pearline on the floor. Violet saw her deformed wrist first. She looked for something to splint the wrist with and settled on heavy cardboard.

"Pearline, curl your fingers around this cardboard, and we'll have a splint until Doc gets here. You're going to need a cast for a few weeks." She then secured it with wide masking tape and started checking Pearline from head to toe.

"Did you fall, Pearline?"

"No, Johnny was here."

Violet's mouth fell open, and Sam jumped up and started looking around to make sure Johnny was gone. Pearline told them of his attack and stealing her money.

"I'll take care of this, Pearline," Sam declared. "Let's get Doc Gerstein out here. You can't stay here by yourself. You need to come and stay with us until this is resolved. Violet, you call Dr. Gerstein."

Violet went to the phone and called. Doc was barely out of the bed. "Doc, Pearline has a broken wrist, and I'm still checking her over. Can you hurry? She'll be at the farm."

"Of course, Violet. I'll bring the supplies for a cast. I'm on the way."

"Sam, help me get Pearline to a chair. I need to put some things in a bag for her to take to our place."

Sam gently pulled Pearline up and pulled a chair over for her to sit in. He hugged her with genuine care.

"Johnny said Sara is next. We have to protect her. He has a look in his eye that he is no longer sane. Do you hear me?" Pearline cried.

"Yes, Pearline. Sheriff Bone said Johnny was doing and saying crazy things while in jail. He talks to someone, and they're not there. He is delusional. We know this is the end. We can't let anyone else get hurt. Now, we need to get you to the car and get you settled in at our house. Just lean on me," Sam encouraged.

Sam went to the back of the property and got C.W. as soon as he had Pearline settled in bed and resting. He shared the morning events. C.W. was livid but calm.

"Let's think this through," he said, while pacing the floor. "What are we going to do? How are we going to take care of this little matter? I need to think. Sam, you go back to the house and keep an eye on everyone. I'll see you in a while."

"Don't you do anything without me. I don't want to find you dead, and I could have helped. Do you understand me, C.W.?"

"Yes, I get it, Sam. This is an opportunity, and we have to do it right."

C.W. showed at the house two hours later. Doc had come and gone, and Pearline was sleeping from the pain medicine. Sara knew she was in danger but stood strong. C.W. hugged her tight. "It will be okay. Do you hear me?"

"I believe you," Sara replied. "Are you going to find Johnny?"

"Today, I feel I want to try to buy some moonshine. I'll go looking for Bart," said C.W. "Sometimes, you have to play along."

C.W. went in on the east side of the property that faced the still. The first movement C.W. saw was Johnny pacing. Every step or two, he would hit himself on the side of the head. He kept repeating, "You're stupid, stupid, stupid." It looked like Johnny was drinking moonshine. He tipped the bottle and drank. He was dancing around singing about whiskey. Something about red makes you dead and what burns blue makes your blues go away. C.W. sat down and watched. Johnny was crazy as a lune.

After watching for an hour, C.W. staggered out of the protection of the tree line waving a few dollar bills. Johnny stood and focused. He stumbled forward as C.W. asked, "Where's Bart? I need to buy a quart of whiskey."

"Well, Bart no longer lives here, and I sell the whiskey now."

"Fine by me. Get me a bottle. I got a twenty for you. Where did Bart go? Start another still down the road?"

"Hell no. He ain't never gonna make moonshine again. I killed him. He's six feet under," slurred Johnny. "I should have done it years ago, after all the times I was locked in that closet and kicked around by him."

"Well, good for you. I'll be needing whiskey every week if I can get it. Is that possible?"

"Sure." Johnny turned and walked off. He returned with a quart of whiskey and took the twenty. C.W. slid into the trees and left the property. Sam had quietly waited in the tree line and heard everything. They looked at each other and walked home.

"What now?" Sam asked.

"Well, that's a good question, but I'm not sure yet," C.W. responded. "I wonder if he buried Bart's body on the property? I'm sure he's dead."

"Does it matter?" Sam asked.

"No, just thinking about everything. Trying to decide my next step. We got whiskey though," C.W. shared and laughed.

At the end of the day, Sam called in the assault to Sheriff Bone. "We're trying to keep you on your toes," Sam said. "I know you don't have enough to do. Johnny assaulted Pearline and broke her arm. You can talk to Dr. Gerstein if you need to confirm the facts."

"Well hell, sounds like we need to take Johnny out of his misery. You don't even know how I wish I could. I'll pick him up today."

"You need to go in on the east side of the property where the still is," Sam said. "He's there on the porch most evenings. Yes, I've been watching him, so I know his routine. That's all I'm going to tell you."

"Well, that says a lot. I'll let you know when I take him in."

CHAPTER 15

C.W. made a call to Sullivan as soon as he left Sam's place. His mind was in turmoil, and he had to act fast for Sara's sake. Sara had grown up right in front of him. She wasn't a child anymore. She was a young woman—a beautiful young woman who men would want. C.W. feared what Johnny's intentions were if he forcefully overcame her.

"Sullivan, I need you to find a two-flat. Sara got accepted for nursing school in Chicago. The other flat will be kept empty for us or if she makes a friend at school. She might want to rent it out for extra money."

"Any particular price range, boss? What side of town?"

"The building will be owned by her. I don't care about the cost. It has to be in a safe area—a good part of town. I want you to hire someone to paint the walls. I'll ask her what color she wants. Get back to me on that. Let me know when you have completed the transaction. Use the same information that you used for her safety deposit box at National Bank. We need to move fast. I also want you to buy furniture for it after the flat is painted. Just the basics. She is going to be very busy when she gets to school."

C.W. changed the subject. "Anything going on at the pub that I need to know about?"

"Seems to be a lot more strangers coming into the pub, and I see a lot of occupied cars outside. A couple of the boys say they're being followed. There's a Buick outside the pub most days until close. We got the plate number, and it's owned by one of the Outfitters. We're watching everything. Back to the furniture. What style?"

"Well, all that surveillance was expected. Don't take care of any bad business at the pub," C.W ordered. "You hear me? As far as furniture, get something modern. I think Sara will welcome some change in her life."

"I'm keeping an eye open. Nothing will go down at the pub." Sullivan hung up and turned to see who could be listening at the bar. It was sparse at this hour of the morning.

C.W. walked back to the farm and gave Violet a big hug.

"You worrying yourself sick?" C.W. asked.

"What do you think? I see the wheels are turning in that little brain of yours, too." Violet smiled at him. C.W.'s eyes widened with feigned shock. "I know Sam is beside himself. Sara is quiet. They're picking tomatoes in the garden for supper. Be ready in about twenty minutes."

C.W. walked to the garden and smiled. "Father and daughter hard at it." There were more tomatoes than they could carry. "You guys need some more hands?" asked C.W.

They both said yes at the same time and smiled back at him. He filled his hands and arms, and they went to supper loaded down.

"Wow, that's quite a few ripe ones today," Violet remarked. "I'll have to make something fast so they don't go to waste. BLT for tomorrow's lunch, stewed tomatoes for supper, and I'll can a few. Well, that fills my week." Violet laughed.

As soon as everyone was settled and plates were full, C.W. set the pace for the conversation. "Sara, I know you will be leaving real soon for nursing school. I found a two-flat on a good side of Chicago. Do you think you would like to see it?"

A huge smile filled Sara's face. "Oh, WOW, yes, I would. I don't want to live in the dorm if I don't have to. I hear we work long hours anyway, and I kind of want to get away from the hospital when I can. What's a two-flat?"

"It's like one house with two apartments. You can live on one side and rent out the other—maybe to another nursing student, or maybe you have a friend going to school there, too," C.W. said. "They are going to put a fresh coat of paint on the walls. What color do you want?"

"Oh gosh. I never thought about paint. How about a smoky blue? This is so exciting."

Sam was quiet. He didn't want to deal with this right now, but it would get Sara to safety.

C.W. looked at Sam. "After it's painted and the furniture is delivered, I thought you could go see it. Violet, too. You could drive up together, stay for the weekend at the flat, and check out the hospital where Sara will be working and training. What do you think?"

Sam smiled. "That I can deal with. Violet, you need a day or two away. This way, we will both have an idea of where she is. What do you think?"

"I am so ready," Violet said. "Well, not for Sara to go away to school, but a weekend away would be good. Let's plan on it as soon as the flat is ready. Thanks for taking care of that for Sara."

"I always said I would and now, it's almost a done deal. I'll pay for the schooling, too. Sara, you will be a great nurse with what you have learned from Violet, and what you have been doing with the neighbors," C.W. said, with pride in his voice. "You'll definitely know more about herbal medicine than they do. Maybe you can teach them something." They all laughed.

CHAPTER 16

C.W. farmed the next day while Sam, Violet, and Sara went to town for supplies and groceries.

"I like coming to town," Sara commented. "It's an all-day deal, and we get to eat out. Not that your food isn't delicious, Grandma."

"I know what you mean, child. I kind of like it myself. It's good to get away and look around. Breaks the monotony of farm life. It's a treat for all of us. I'm starving for hamburgers, fries, and cherry cokes at the diner," said Violet.

When they were done eating, Sam laughed. "I should have ordered two burgers," he said. "That was delicious." Afterwards, Sam headed for the hardware store while Violet and Sara went grocery shopping. Sam stopped at Sherriff Bone's office to see what had happened with Johnny. Unfortunately, Johnny was nowhere to be found when Sheriff Bone went to their place. Again, they were going to have to be alert. They had to find Johnny before he found Sara.

When they got out of the car at the farm, they each grabbed a bag of groceries. Sara called Sheba as she walked. Sheba didn't come. C.W. said he hadn't seen her for several hours. Something wasn't right. Sheba always came bounding to the car when they returned. She stayed close to the house.

"Sheba!" Sara cried out. No response. Sam could see how distraught Sara was. Sam got on the tractor and pulled Sara up to sit on the wheel well. "Let's see if we can find her."

They headed for the back of the property. They rode miles looking. They trampled the woods and went on foot for miles. They called her name until they were hoarse. They came to the pond, and Sam waded in and spread the cattails. Sam prayed they wouldn't find Sheba under those circumstances. It would be devastating for all of them.

C.W. headed for the land surrounding Johnny's place. He walked slowly and quietly, listening for anything unusual. He was beginning to question whether someone had poisoned her. He didn't think Sheba would take food or water from anyone though. He walked on. He was now in the neighbor's fields looking in barns, outhouses, and chicken coops. He didn't leave anywhere unturned. He walked back to Sam's. He went through the trash piles behind the shop and lifted old tires and parts.

They all met back at the house at the same time. Violet had been calling neighbors. No one had seen Sheba. It was dusk. The boys and Sara all had their guns strapped on. Tears were streaming down Sara's face. She felt more helpless as the day turned into night. Sara was determined. She knew Sheba would find her if she were missing.

"By God, I will find you Sheba," Sara proclaimed. There wasn't even a chance Sara was going to bed. She put on her jeans and hoodie and told C.W. and Sam she was going to Johnny's to listen from their wooded area. There was no stopping her, so they all went. They sat within the tree line for an hour. No one spoke. Then, there was the faintest of cries. Almost a whimper. Sara crawled to the edge of the property. Sam and C.W. were right behind her.

"Let's all go a different direction," Sara said.

C.W. didn't want to do that. He spoke quietly. "I'll go by the still. Sam, you go to the barn."

"I'm going to the area before Pearl's place where all the junk is," Sara proclaimed. She quietly slipped away from them, sliding down the bank beside the gravel road. She listened intensely for the whimper. After twenty minutes, she heard it again. There were old cars, trucks, and wash tubs surrounding her. Sara thought she heard something. A movement. She went to the ground and waited. Nothing else came. Only stillness now. Sara walked on, hiding and crouching in the weeds as she went. She heard a mournful whine and followed the sound. Now, it sounded like a baby.

Sara pulled out her flashlight and looked through the brush and junk. Inside was a doghouse. She ran for it and dropped to her knees, then flipped the switch to the light ever so briefly and saw the blood on the doghouse. Her heart was pounding. She crawled in the doghouse. Sheba had been beaten and was bleeding. Sara felt desperate. How was she going to get C.W. or her dad to help her?

Sara kept checking Sheba and looked at cuts on her ribs and face. Her right rear leg looked deformed. Sheba was too weak to lift her head or respond as Sara whispered to her. There was a belt so tight around her neck, Sheba could hardly breathe.

Working quickly, Sara finally released the belt. As she backed out of the doghouse, a hand went over her mouth, and she was drawn tight to someone's body. She fumbled for her gun, trying to scream, then kicked for all she was worth.

Sam whispered, "Be quiet, Sara, or we'll get shot." He kept her mouth covered and turned her around. Sara collapsed against her father for a brief moment. "Hurry, help me," she said. "Sheba is dying."

Sam went down on his knees and drug Sheba out. He gently picked her up and started for the house. "Sara, have your gun ready. I saw Johnny, and he is packing. He's also drunk."

"I've got it, Dad." Sara kept talking to Sheba softly. "We got you, Sheba. You're going to be okay." Sara saw C.W. in the distance and flashed the light on and off. Their heart ached to see what Johnny had done to Sheba.

C.W. saw Sheba and took his jacket off. He wrapped Sheba into a papoose and carried her the rest of the way. "I feel so bad for Sheba," C.W. stated. "Johnny's day is coming. I promise you that."

As soon as they got to the farm, Grandma was there waiting. She saw Sheba and ran for the medicine bag. "Sara, get a baby bottle and fill it with water. Sheba's dehydrated."

Sara rubbed Sheba's throat, praying she would swallow as she offered small amounts of water.

Grandma tended to all her open wounds and put ointment on them. Sam massaged her all over to increase circulation, then called the vet. He immobilized Sheba's leg, not knowing whether it was the leg or the hip.

"Violet, do you think it's broken or dislocated?"

Violet just shook her head as she continued caring for Sheba's wounds. Sheba had swallowed, and they were all thrilled. Sara kept giving small amounts of water. The vet arrived, and C.W. slid out of the picture. Sam shared what had happened and how long Sheba had been missing.

"You're lucky you got her when you did. A few more hours, and it would have been a different story," the vet said. "Sheba's hip is dislocated, and I have to manipulate it."

Sheba didn't make a sound. She was exhausted and weak.

"I have immobilized the hip and have administered some antibiotics to prevent infection," the vet said. "Sheba's lungs are clear. In forty-eight hours, Sheba should be eating and trying to get up. If you need anything, call me in the morning and I'll come back."

Sam shook his hand as he prepared to leave, then walked him out.

C.W. reappeared the minute the vet left. He sat on the floor and cradled Sheba's head and rubbed her ever so gently. Sam came through the door and sat beside them. Sara and Violet also gathered around Sheba. They would never know how Johnny had tricked Sheba. They *did* know it was payback for the day Sheba had jumped through the screen and tore his hand to pieces.

"I have had enough," Sam said.

"I agree," C.W. replied. "What do we do with a mentally ill kid who just keeps hurting those around him? Where can he go? Is there an institution he can be admitted to?"

"I'll see what Sheriff Bone says in the morning. I'm going to stay close to Sheba tonight," Sam said.

"I will, too," Sara declared.

"Well, don't think you're getting rid of me," C.W. said, laughing.

"Well, I think Sheba is in good hands, so I'm going to bed," Violet announced. She slipped away to her bedroom. She was thinking, *I'm too old for all this excitement.* Sleep came easy.

Again, Johnny was nowhere to be found. Sam had notified Sheriff Bone, and they had both gone to the property. The still was quiet now. Sam walked to the doghouse and showed the sheriff where everything had taken place. By now, Johnny knew Sheba was gone. Little did he know, C.W. would be looking for him. He wouldn't stop until Johnny was stopped. Sam knew in his soul that when someone hurt Sara, C.W. was ruthless. It was a matter of time. C.W. was already headed for the Medlar property. He was looking at every inch of the land and under everything as well.

C.W. entered the barn and went to the loft. Nothing had been there for years. No equipment lined the wall and there was nothing in storage. The only thing present was what appeared to be old, dried blood. The property was visible through the cracks of the walls.

C.W. scanned around and saw no movement. He descended the old stairs from the loft and headed to another building that was barely standing. It was barren. The kudzu could hide anything. He wouldn't know whether he was being watched. He and Sara had experienced that a few months ago.

C.W. hated that Sheba had been beaten. She must have been taken off guard. It was almost impossible to slip up on her with her patrol training. Something out of the ordinary had definitely occurred. The injury to her jaw was probably from a head contusion that stunned her.

C.W. knew today was not going to be the day he found Johnny. Disappointed, he headed back to the house to check on Sheba. When he walked in, Sheba lifted her head and licked his hand. He sat down beside her, then proceeded to rub her shoulders, staying clear of her hip. She was taking water well and had eaten that morning.

"Violet, do we need anything for Sheba?"

"No, she had a few bites of dog food this morning. That's a good sign. I dressed her wounds earlier. They look good. She will heal pretty fast now. She's trying to sit up. Probably knows she can't lie there much longer or she will stiffen up. Sheba is smart. She'll be up in a few hours. I'll keep an eye on her if you need to do something with Sam. I'm doing laundry today. You need anything washed?"

"I'll go to the house and bring a few things. I'm down to my last pair of socks. Things will be smelling pretty rank if I don't get some clean ones," C.W. said, chuckling. Violet just shook her head and wrinkled her nose.

"Sara went to bed early this morning. She stayed up all night watching Sheba. She lay right beside her on the floor."

"I knew she would. Sara loves that dog," C.W. responded, as he left to get his clothes. When he got to the farm, Sullivan was there waiting on him.

CHAPTER 17

"**B**oss, there's a war going on in Chicago. After we hit the warehouse, I told you there was always a car outside, and we felt we were being watched. Last night, Ted was hit. Hit bad. Hit twice in the thigh. Missed the femoral artery or he would be dead. One bullet creased his skull, and he has a concussion. No bullets lodged in him. They're out for blood."

"How can you be sure what their plan is?" asked C.W.

I recognized one of the guys. He was an army veteran. I saved his ass in the war. He's loyal to me for that. I won't risk his life, though. He told me if they find a connection between us, he will lose his job and his life. We've made a good life bootlegging."

"What's really troubling you, Sullivan?"

"We're watching our backs twenty-four-seven. We are losing our boys."

"I know I have had distractions here with Sara. You boys need to follow my orders."

"You forget our defeats by death. Your scheme is slow, and we are like sitting ducks now," Sullivan said.

C.W. smiled at Sullivan in confidence. "I have made you rich and shared my profits. Times are tough now because of our wars on the streets. I will not fail. I think you have grown weary in my absence. I will return to Chicago late tonight. I'm asking you to trust me as you always have."

Sullivan stood tall, and a slow grin creased his handsome face. "We're always better with you at the bar. You are the glue. Being gone too long gives the boys doubts. Seems to be more guys on the docks by the warehouse, so I don't approach it at all. I think our competition has sentries at multiple locations. They're waiting and watching to see who passes and what is going down."

Sara interrupted the conversation as she came to a halt and jumped from her bicycle. "Hello, Sullivan." She had met Sullivan a year ago when he had delivered a package to her.

"It's good to see you again, Sara. You've grown up," Sullivan said with a smile.

"Yes, older and wiser. Maybe leery of the world." Sara smiled at Sullivan, then turned to C.W., who hugged her in greeting. "This can only mean you have to leave and go back to Chicago. Am I right?" she asked him.

"Yes, Sara. It is time I got back to Chicago," C.W. confirmed. "I'll come back if you need me for anything. Remember all I taught you about shooting, and always carry your gun. Especially now that Johnny is getting sicker." He hugged her again, tight.

Sullivan left to head back to Chicago, and C.W. and Sara headed for the house. They walked with their arms around each other. "Sheba is getting up now. It hurts for her to take a step, but she does anyway. Just very slow. She's in a lot of pain," Sara said.

"I know, but she is strong and will recover in two weeks. She can do it. Johnny will never get anything over on her again. This time, it had to be very devious and with intent. I think he hit her in the head and stunned her. He was probably waiting on her. That will be the only time Johnny hurts her."

C.W. left that evening following dinner. It was a grim meal. Sheba beaten, and now he had to leave. Back in Chicago, C.W. drove within sight of the bar and parked the car. He looked at every car parked and scanned his surroundings for anyone in the shadows. He swaggered down the far side of the sidewalk to a bench that lined up with the front door of the bar. It was in a shadow and just far enough to offer sanctuary. He could see what cars were occupied and who was coming and going in the club.

There was a faint sound of music when the door to the bar opened. An old geezer stumbled towards C.W., who was now on high alert. Sometimes, it's all an act to get close to someone or someplace without drawing too much attention. A street sweeper rolled by. As the drunk approached, C.W. could see he wasn't as old as he'd thought. His face was bruised and scratched up. Obviously, a rough life. As he passed, C.W. nodded. Then, two teenage boys feeling their oats ran past him. C.W. entered the bar after an hour of observing.

"Welcome back, C.W.," said Martin. One of the women chimed in. "What a pleasure to have you back." A well-dressed man came and shook his hand. C.W. made his way across the bar. He was stopped repeatedly for small talk and recognition. Sullivan came out of the back to see what the commotion was all about and smiled when he saw C.W.

They shook hands firmly. "Good number of customers for a Thursday night," C.W. said.

"It's been a lot busier the last month. More women are coming in, and that draws the men. I think they are looking for you," Sullivan said, laughing.

"Right. Do you think we can get to the warehouse? Are the docks all being guarded and we shouldn't be seen there?" asked C.W.

"We'll see," Sullivan commented. "It is never the same. I often drive by, and no one is to be seen. Other nights, it's like Grand Central. I need to show you where the action is on the docks now. Power has changed hands again. That way you can see who moved in."

The moon cast shadows as they reached the docks. The water glistened. The warehouse was dark—each side appeared deserted and deathly quiet. "Let's try to see who owns these warehouses that sandwich us. We might need them some day."

"Will do." Sullivan shone his light on the door and unlocked it. As they entered, C.W. marveled at the number of barrels of pure grain alcohol along with crates of weapons. The warehouse was secure. They left to return to the bar.

They had barely entered the door when a fight broke out—two strangers to the bar who reeked of whiskey. The fight seemed staged and was over before it had truly started. C.W. strode over. "Who do you boys work for?"

"Hell, we do odd jobs at the dock. Just blowing off steam."

"Where'd you come from?" asked C.W.

"Right here in Chicago—southside. Lived here all our lives."

C.W. could see they were backpedaling, but no harm done.

"Well, thanks for coming in, boys. Let's keep the fights out of the bar." C.W. walked away. Sullivan watched and was ready for any move they might make.

The next day, C.W. and Sullivan dressed in work clothes as a disguise and returned to the docks. They were just gathering information on where the booze was stashed and if it was for the taking. Seeing who was working for whom. They fit in perfectly. They were just another dock worker and even actually moved a few crates while asking questions. The warehouse that housed the whiskey was farther down the docks. That was a good thing. C.W. wanted it away from his warehouse.

They saw a number of cops. Half of them were on the take. He and Sullivan sauntered on down the docks, and as they got closer to the whiskey, the toughs became more abundant. Some were at the entrance, the loading docks, and even between the warehouses. The boys were moving fast as they unloaded the goods. As they walked by the doors to the warehouse, they could see the boys had their guns out.

"Hey, man, what are you doing on our dock?" asked the hood.

"Well, we're just looking for a fast buck. We worked the docks before and needed some cash. Marco, down at the next block, said you might be hiring," C.W. responded.

The hood's mouth twisted into a grim smile as he responded. "Hell, we can always use help."

Sullivan and C.W. stopped walking. "Where do we sign up?" C.W. asked.

The hood motioned for them to see the man inside. They entered the warehouse and saw liquor, whiskey, firearms, and more. It was payday. All of a sudden, there was shouting on the dock, and everyone headed that direction. C.W. and Sullivan just walked away. They had what they had come after.

"Okay," C.W. commented, as they were driving away. "We're going to have to see how many boys are on the docks after midnight. No one was in the back of the warehouse. How many men do we need to take to case the joint after 3 a.m.?" They were headed south towards the bar.

"Probably seven to be safe," said Sullivan. "Need one at every angle of the building for lookouts. We definitely need Elliott and Martin. They're good at hiding themselves. Junior's good at scaling a building and getting in the windows. Toni is just an animal, so he can lead the pack."

It was already after one, so there wouldn't be any sleep that night. Sullivan called the boys to the office and sketched out the building and entrances. Questions were answered, and the plan was on. At 3 a.m., they loaded into two trucks and parked closer to their warehouse than the one they were hitting. Toni went first, and the bolt cutters did quick work on the lock. The gates were open. There was one guard at the front of the warehouse, and Toni put him out of commission in under ten seconds. He was a small, well-built guy, but meaner than a junkyard dog.

The boys crept in. There was no one else in the warehouse. "Either they're letting their guard down, or they're just stupid," said Sullivan.

"Don't get cocky," ordered C.W. "Get the trucks in here. Those dock workers start early, and I'm not going to be here to greet them or serve them coffee. Move it."

Sullivan signaled one of the guards. The two large, black delivery trucks pulled into the warehouse and killed the engines. Toni and C.W. loaded one truck while Sullivan and Junior loaded the second truck. The gun crates were loaded last.

"Done," yelled C.W. "Move these trucks down the dock. No lights. Get the trucks in our warehouse. There can be no activity on the docks and no noise. Do you understand?"

"Yes, boss."

The trucks rolled out slowly. They left the doors ajar, and the trucks disappeared in a matter of minutes within their new warehouse.

C.W. barked, "Get these trucks unloaded. We have maybe one hour. Otherwise, we have to leave the trucks here. It would be better if the trucks were nowhere on the dock."

Sullivan looked at C.W. "You're losing your cool, man."

"No, I'm not. This could be it," said C.W. "I'm distracted. Sara is getting ready to move to Chicago. I won't be doing any of this while she's here." He could see her face as he worked. "I can't make any mistakes with her in town. Starting tonight, we will have surveillance around the bar. Nothing can go wrong. I will probably post a man in the warehouse, too. No one is to breathe a word to anyone about this heist. Understood?"

"You think someone's automatically coming to the bar, suspecting us?" asked Sullivan.

"Crazier things have happened, and I'm not going to be caught off guard. Too much to lose. We have hundreds of thousands of their property in our warehouse. We already robbed them once. Yes, I think they may come around looking. You know I get these gut feelings. I pay attention to those feelings," said C.W.

As soon as the trucks were unloaded, the merchandise was covered with tarps. It was still early, and the trucks were removed from the docks in the dark. The wind had picked up, and they were exposed. They didn't see anyone, but that didn't mean they weren't seen leaving.

The trucks were wiped down and left at a lot twenty blocks from the bar. The crew walked in the back alley to the bar and entered through the rear door. C.W. set up whiskey for the boys. A card game started, and they finally left in the wee hours of the morning. Guards were on duty before they left.

Everyone was back at the bar the following night. There was a private card game going on in the back room behind the hidden panel. C.W. was restless and left the bar, walking and watching. Nothing was out of the ordinary. Then he went to the car and drove east to the flat he had purchased for Sara. He went in and sat down in the dark and thought. For some reason, he was wanting to leave this city, but not while Sara was going to school. He would be there to help her if she needed him. Maybe it would be the other way around, and he would need her. Lately, he had been thinking a lot about his life. The farm—his home, and always Violet and Sam. He finally realized he would rather be there. But Sara was coming to Chicago, so one more year. Then, he was throwing in the towel and getting out of the business.

He fell asleep until 9 a.m. When he woke, he showered in the second flat and headed out to the bar. He needed to get his business and financials in order.

The rumors were everywhere he went. Gossip about the warehouse, the booze, and the guns. All kinds of speculation about who had taken them from the mob and not a trace of information leading to the culprits. Sullivan couldn't believe the word had gotten out so fast. He kept watching the door the following weeks.

Two weeks later, the door to the bar quietly opened. In walked two of the mob dressed in their pinstripe suits and fedoras worn low. *Peculiar to be so obvious,* thought Sullivan. They were direct, but not obnoxious. Watching their faces, he knew they were looking for information. After some small talk with some of the customers and a couple of drinks, they left as quietly as they had come, heading for the next bar on the block.

C.W. had watched it all from behind the hidden panels in the wall.

"So, what are we going to do?" asked Sullivan.

"Nothing," C.W. responded. "They didn't get any information. They're fishing. The warehouse is unknown. The liquor can't be found, and that's how it will remain for six to twelve months. It's just an asset now. Let's go grab some lunch and get out of here a while. There's some loose details regarding the mob that we need to find out about."

They played cards in three pubs that day. No one knew anything about who had done the heist, but the mob was out looking in full force. Next, they walked to the docks and just hung out. Everyone was looking for information that day. Finally, they headed back to the bar on foot.

"I'm returning to the farm tonight," C.W. said quietly. "I'll be gone for a few weeks. I have unfinished business regarding a kid who keeps antagonizing my family. I have to put an end to it, or there will never be peace and comfort on the farm again. Sara's life depends on me."

"Okay, I'll let you know if anything changes here. I don't think it will," responded Sullivan.

C.W. left the minute they got to the bar.

CHAPTER 18

C.W. rolled into Violet's farmhouse from the east side of the property. He didn't want to wake anyone or prolong their evening. Sam would stay up for hours talking about C.W.'s latest adventures. Sara and Violet as well. For some reason, C.W. was in a mood. He felt lonely, but was here with his family a few hundred feet through the fields. Contemplation kept him occupied as he unpacked his minimal belongings. The long, hard thinking about Johnny had him worried. Should Johnny disappear? Hang him? Beat him? C.W.'s biggest concern was how Sara and Sam would feel if he did any of those things to Johnny.

He quietly left the house and walked to the Medlar property, pondering his options. A few minutes later, he observed a car roll into the property for whiskey. C.W. watched Johnny as he took the money, and the sedan rolled out. Johnny went back to working the still.

C.W. briskly walked away in the patches of woods.

Morning came too soon, but he was hungry. He jumped out of bed and dressed. Breakfast sounded good, and C.W. was starving. He saw Sam at the corncrib, and a smile from Sam was welcome enough. He got a slap on the back as well. "Did you come in late last night?" Sam asked.

"I wanted to check on Sara and Sheba. That whole mess still has me worried. Are they okay?"

"Sara's cautious, and Sheba is back to her old self. They have taken some walks, and Sheba chased a rabbit or two. She had a grey wolf cornered a few days ago, but I called her off. Wasn't harming anything. There's less and less wolves here," shared Sam.

"Good to hear she's not still down or hurt permanently. Sara was beside herself that night. She's become quite attached to Sheba," C.W. commented.

"That's for sure," Sam agreed. "She doesn't let her out of her sight now. Let's get some breakfast."

"It's about time you got here, C.W.," Violet said when they walked in. "You got banker's hours now?" Violet laughed as she greeted him and gave him a hug. She passed the bacon. Sam was already digging in and was on his third cup of coffee.

"Is Sara sleeping in today?" asked C.W.

"No, I'm surprised you didn't see her and Sheba. I needed a digitalis plant to make a tea for John Thomas, and she offered to get it in the woods. He's got an irregular heartbeat, and we thought we'd try this remedy first. She should be back any minute," Sam said. "I have to work on the tractor. Can you help me when you finish, C.W.? It goes a lot faster with a second set of hands."

"Sure. I'll be out in just a few minutes."

Sam headed for the barn. He saw Sara in the distance, and Sheba was running toward him. Sam reached down and rough-housed with Sheba a few minutes. Sara headed on towards the house after a wave, and Sheba stayed with him.

"As always, that was delicious, Violet. Now my belly is full, I can hardly walk, and Sam wants me to work," C.W. whined. "What's wrong with that picture?"

"Oh shoo. Get to work, and stop your complaining," Violet said, as she swatted C.W. with the dishtowel. He ran for the back door.

C.W. stepped out the back door to bright sun blinding him. But, in that brief second from shadow to light, he caught a glimpse or the blur of something or someone to his right. Fear overtook him. He saw Johnny just a few feet behind Sara. She was straining with arms and legs pumping trying to outrun Johnny and distance herself. Unfortunately, between fragility and asthma, she was losing the race.

C.W. saw Johnny lurch forward, arm outstretched, and his fingers curled around Sara's ponytail. He took a handful of hair and his grip tightened. Sara's head was drawn back. As Johnny slammed his hands to the earth, Sara's body looked like an accordion in motion. Her body slammed into the hard ground between the rows of corn, where the silk tassels were blowing gently. C.W. tore into the sunlight. He destroyed the garden as he uprooted plants. He was running to help the most important person in his life.

Johnny was leaning over Sara, oblivious to C.W.'s approach. He tore Sara's shirt and stared at her glossy, smooth skin, so warm and soft beneath his fingertips. The voices were back, telling him to touch her, to hurt her. She had to pay.

Before C.W. could reach Sara, he saw Sheba's sleek, muscular frame soaring through the air. Fangs bared, shackles up, and with a growl that would cause fear in any sane man, Sheba crashed into Johnny from behind, mauling his face and left ear. C.W. knelt beside Sara and closed her shirt, realizing at the same time that she wasn't breathing. C.W. only had a short time to save her life. He tilted Sara's head back and gave two quick breaths in her mouth as he pinched her nose tight. He started pumping her chest. He needed a flat surface. He needed help. He took out his .45 and fired twice. Violet ran out the door, saw Sara down, and turned to retrieve a vial and a syringe. Violet ran through the garden. She could see Sam rolling in on the tractor, which was smoking and rattling like the engine would explode.

Once Violet reached Sara, she injected the epinephrine with trembling hands. Seconds later, Sara was wheezing, skin diaphoretic, and color ashen. Her lips were blue.

Sheba was on guard, straddling Johnny. C.W. stood and walked over to Johnny when Violet and Sam arrived.

"You bastard. How dare you come on our land and attack Sara. She never hurt anyone in her life." Johnny wanted to run but could barely crawl. Sheba had done a number on him. He had deep gashes from Sheba all over his body. His ear was hanging, and his face was torn open. Sheba had barely missed his jugular.

C.W. yanked Johnny to his feet and struck him in the face repeatedly. The first blow was to his open cheekbone, and the second, to his nose. His fists kept coming. C.W. wanted him dead. "Paybacks are hell, aren't they, Johnny," C.W. spat.

Johnny had his arms out in front as though he could ward off blows from C.W.

Meanwhile, Sheba was licking Sara's face and nudging her. Sam picked up Sara and ran for the house, with Violet close behind. They placed her on the bed, turned the fan on her, and started rubbing her face and neck with a cool cloth. Finally, a gasp erupted from Sara. It was like a swimmer on his last leg. Her whole body was straining to get out of the black hole. Her eyes opened, and her breathing improved with each gasp for air. Her color was returning, and she was no longer sucking air.

Violet was by her side. "You're okay," she said. "Calm your breathing."

Sara listened to her voice and followed the directive. Finally, her breathing came easier. Sara felt like a poker had gone through her chest. She tried to raise herself, but Violet gently pushed her down on the pillow. Sara was shaking from the exertion from trying to sit up. "You have to rest. I'll get you some tea."

Sam ran back to the field as soon as Violet returned. "STOP, C.W. You've almost killed him. Sheriff Bone is on the way. Johnny will be behind bars for this."

C.W. rose from the ground and walked away, trying to get a grip on his rage and fear. He couldn't comprehend the hatred from Johnny towards this beautiful girl whom he loved as a daughter. He didn't want Sam to see him crying, but that's exactly what he did.

Deep sobs came from him as never before. Sam followed and put his arms around C.W.

"I know you love her as much as I do. You helped bring her into this world. I will never be able to repay you for everything you have done for her." They were silent for the longest time. Brothers through it all.

C.W. stayed in the back bedroom when Sheriff Bone arrived. No one the wiser that he was even there.

When it was all said and done, Johnny went to prison for twenty years for attempted murder. He sat in the courtroom rocking and talking to himself. Pearl testified, and so did Tim, that they'd heard Johnny threaten to kill Sara. Sam and Violet testified to all of his assaults and stalking of Sara over the years. The assault of Pearl came out as well. Sheriff Bone testified to his mental status while in jail.

Sara got stronger as the days passed but stayed closer to home now. She startled easily and heard every noise in the old house. Pearline was now coming to see her and bringing books as well. Sam was worried and watched her constantly. Violet saw her staring out the windows and scanning the horizon past the fields. "Sara, do you want to talk?" Violet asked.

"No, Grandma, I'm just thinking."

"I thought I heard some wheels turning," Violet replied, smiling. "I think you can't stop looking for Johnny, but he's not coming back. I know you know that."

"I'll get past it all. I guess he scared me. I'm really weak when it comes down to protecting myself. I realize that now. I'm haunted by Johnny."

"He took you by surprise. It could have been worse, but Sheba saved the day. C.W. saved your life."

"I know. I have to tell him thank you. I just haven't been myself. I don't think C.W. is coming around because he really wanted to kill

Johnny. Dad stopped him by yelling at him. Well, not *really* yelling at him, but made C.W. realize killing was not the best decision."

"Your dad just knows how to stop C.W. and says the right words. Maybe C.W. feels guilty. He doesn't need to feel guilty. Your dad just believes in honesty and justice in the right way and by the law. He wouldn't change what he said to C.W. We have justice with Johnny in prison. I'm glad we didn't have to bury Johnny, cover up the murder, and live with it forever.

"C.W. has been working on my old house. It needed a lot of repairs and has been neglected for years. Why don't you go and admire his work? It looks beautiful. Willis helps him in the afternoon."

"I didn't know that, Grandma. I thought he went back to Chicago. I'll go right now and talk to him."

Violet put her arms around Sara. "This, too, will pass, child. I am grateful we didn't have to bury Johnny just as much as you. Go talk to C.W. and tell him you love him and thank him. Okay?"

"I will."

Sara walked with Sheba to the old house. C.W. actually saw her coming and ran to meet her. The bear hug went on forever, with Sheba barking and jumping around them.

"I'm really glad to see you, Sara. Come look at the work Willis and I have finished in the kitchen."

"It's beautiful. I love the countertops. You sure surprise me. I know Willis is learning a lot from you. He still has to farm to make ends meet.

"I wanted to thank you for saving me, C.W. If you hadn't walked outside at that very moment, this would have turned out different. I might be dead or raped. No telling what his intention was."

"I know. I was going to kill Johnny. Your dad stopped me, and I'm glad deep down." C.W. felt himself changing, and it was because of Sara. He felt something solid, something permanent, breaking inside him. He was tired of the gangster life and wanted to be with Sara and his family more.

CHAPTER 19

"I feel better, C.W. I'm doing things again and going to see Pearline. She's better, too. Things are happening fast here. It's almost time to go to Chicago and start school. C.W., thank you again for saving my life. I'm forever grateful you love me unconditionally, just like I love you. Can I come to Chicago now and see where I will be living?"

C.W. was choked up and lowered his head. Sara hugged him. He raised his head. "I can't wait for you to see the house. It's ready when you are. We'll have lunch in several places and get you familiar with Chicago. Make plans to stay the weekend, and bring your dad and Violet. They'll feel better about you being in Chicago if they can see the place."

"I will make plans, and we'll call you before we come. I love you. Stay out of trouble in Chicago. I need you. You're my second dad."

"I know," C.W. said. "I'm working on changing my life. I love you." C.W. beamed with pride.

After several months, Sara regained her strength and poise. Even her sense of humor returned. The color bloomed once again in her cheeks. Her laughter was like gold to the family. Sheba and Sara continued taking walks. Of course, she had her gun holstered each time.

Sam came in from the field and showered. Supper was good. Sara's appetite had not been affected, but probably because Violet fixed all her favorites now. "Ladies, it's time we took a trip to Chicago. Sara, your house is ready, and we need to see the school. You need to get familiar with Chicago so you can get around easily. I know you said Patsy was going to school in Chicago, too. Do you want to ask her to go? You can see if she wants to stay with you. It's good to have a roommate. What do you think?"

"Oh, Dad, that would be great. I'll call Patsy. I need a change. This is what the doctor ordered. I can't wait to start school," Sara replied. Sara ran for the phone. Violet smiled.

"Patsy, it's Sara. The greatest thing has happened. My uncle got me a two-flat in Chicago so I don't have to live in the dorm. Do you think you might like to be roommates and then walk to class? Or drive?" Sara laughed.

"That would be great. I really don't want to live with a dozen other girls, sharing the bathroom, and taking turns. When are you going?"

"Well, Dad, Grandma, and I thought about driving up for the weekend. Maybe leave real early Thursday morning and come back early Sunday morning. Then, we can see the flat, see the school, and get familiar with restaurants and stores. Ask your parents if you can go with us." The excitement emanated from Sara.

"Okay, I will. This is great," Patsy squealed. "I'll call you later. Dad's not home."

Sam had just laid down when he heard a soft scratching at the door. Sara's trademark. Sam pushed back the covers and strode to the door. He pulled the door open, and Sara went to his arms, as she had so many times before. He just held her. No words necessary. Sheba sat looking up at them. "Look, Sheba is jealous."

"No, she isn't, she knows I love her, too. She just wants some affection," Sara replied. "Love you, Dad. Good night." Sara turned to Sheba. "Come on," she said, then turned back to Sam. "Oh, I forgot to tell you Patsy is asking her parents if she can go with us to Chicago. She really wants to stay in the house and be roommates. I'm really excited."

"Me, too. It will be a great time for you both. Love you, too."

The day finally arrived. It was 6 a.m., and they were in front of Patsy's house. She was ready and running down the steps with an overnight bag. Her father waved from the porch, and Sam waved back. They were off for Chicago. The girls chattered most of the way. The day was clear and ideal for a road trip.

Sam was driving slowly, as they reached the outskirts of Chicago. The streets were neat and clean. Then, an array of businesses and stores popped up. As they got closer to downtown, it became more prosperous. Michigan Avenue was busy. The girls were in awe of SAKS FIFTH AVENUE. Some stores had taste and style and others were drab and boring.

"Look, Patsy, we can shop at Saks." The Allerton Hotel put them in awe. "Oh my gosh, there's Blum's Vogue and Main Street Bookstore. We have to go there," Sara exclaimed. Sara had been reading about Chicago and intended to see it all. Then, they were on State Street, and it was something else. The hustle and bustle made you excited that you were there. The flags hung on most buildings in reverence to their fine country. Cars were bumper-to-bumper. The lights were stately as they bent over the streets. The bars and liquor stores were lined up. Sam turned off.

They pulled off the street and stopped in front of the two-flat. The sun hit the brick, giving it a glowing warmth. Sara jumped out of the car and ran towards the house. There was a front porch and lots of steps. The bay window was new to Sara. As she started up the steps, the door opened, and there was C.W. She jumped in his arms, and he hugged her tight. "You look wonderful, Sara. I've been so worried about you."

"C.W., this is my girlfriend, Patsy. She's going to nursing school, too. I think she will room with me."

C.W. extended his hand, and they shook. "I'm glad you are going to room together. It's always good to have a friend with you."

Patsy smiled and marveled at the house. Sara and Patsy sat in the bay window at the same time and started laughing as they watched people coming and going. The girls chattered endlessly with excitement. It was going to be great.

The girls went to look at the second flat. "C.W., why does this flat have beds and furniture, too?

"Well, sweetheart, I may want to spend more time close to you, and I will have a place right next door to you. I can sleep here, if I want, and we can have dinner together or explore Chicago when you can get away from school."

"I would love that," said Sara, as she jumped up and down smiling.

"Violet, get up here and give me a hug," C.W. said.

"I'd love to, C.W., but these old legs and bones don't move that fast." He met her and took her hand until they reached the porch. Violet turned and gave him a bear hug, then walked in. I can see these girls are going to enjoy living here. Good choice, C.W." Violet walked through the house and ran her hand over the beautiful woodwork. The rooms were huge, and each room had a radiator.

Sam took the steps two at a time and slapped C.W. on the back while they shook hands. Always brothers through thick and thin. "Man, this is a nice neighborhood. Looks like a lot of families live here," Sam shared. They walked through the flat and admired the built-in cabinets. Then, the boys went and sat on the stoop, watching everyone go by and catching up. Several neighbors greeted them as they walked by. "There sure isn't more than walking room between the houses. Guess you can yell for help easier," Sam said, laughing.

Everyone was hungry by that time, and the decision was made to go to Gino's East. It was Sara and Patsy's first deep dish pizza. It would be a first of many other firsts.

They all piled into the car and turned around, heading for Michigan Avenue. "Let's talk some trivia," said C.W. "Where does the term 'windy city' come from?"

Patsy was the first taker. "From the wind coming in off Lake Michigan."

"That's good, but it actually refers to boastful politicians and the fact that they were 'full of hot air,'" said C.W. "Now, when was the Great Chicago Fire?"

"1871," Sam chimed in.

"That is correct. Now, does Chicago turn its rivers green for St. Patrick's Day?"

They all chimed in, "Yes."

"All right, now let's get to the Adler Planetarium." C.W. pointed to the right as Sam drove.

The exhibits were astounding. They spent an hour at the telescope and the star projector. Sara was ecstatic. "The sky is so realistic. I will come back here." Sara loved Chicago already.

"All right, all. It's been a full day, and we need to head for the house. Everyone can try out the beds. Sam, I have a couple of beds for us in the other apartment. Violet, I'll let you stay with the girls."

"Thanks, C.W., but I will fall asleep no matter the type of bed. These girls will be too excited to sleep for a while, and I am sure the TV will keep them busy. Don't be sneaking out, boys."

"Not us. It's been a full day. See you in the morning, and we will head for the school. Goodnight, everyone," C.W. called out, as he and Sam headed for the second flat.

C.W. was up early the next morning and had pancakes and coffee ready. Sam laughed and said, "C.W., are you getting domestic on me? Are you starting to change your ways and settle down to a family life?"

"Well, I'm thinking about it. Violet always cooks for me. So, I thought I would surprise you. Don't get carried away with settling down."

Sara walked in half-asleep.

"After all, Sara is the only girl I think of."

"C.W., I know that's a lie," Sara said, laughing. "You probably have half the women in town after you. I wish you *would* settle down. Breakfast looks awesome, and I'm starving."

C.W. stepped around the table and hugged her fondly.

Everyone was ready in an hour and headed for Polk Street. Cook County School of Nursing worked closely with Cook County Hospital. This gave hands-on experience in all aspects of nursing while assisting the hospital with staffing needs.

As they pulled into the parking lot, it appeared to be an enormous campus. A huge, overpowering, gothic building stood centrally. Signs pointed to pediatrics, psychiatry, infectious disease, outpatient, research, the library, and so much more. It was almost overwhelming. "Look!" Sara exclaimed. "There's the school. It's attached to the hospital. Patsy, look there are nurses' housing and physician residences also. I am so glad we will be at the house."

"Wow, this is huge. I will be exhausted walking from one end to the other." Patsy laughed. They parked and started walking to the administration building.

Quietly, Violet commented to Sam, "I think maybe the girls need to go in and introduce themselves. Maybe go on a tour, and we can wait in the courtyard. It's time we let her be in charge, but we'll be here if she needs us. She is growing up, Sam."

"I was thinking the same thing, Violet. I know you're right."

They all entered and got the girls to the right place.

"Girls, why don't you go introduce yourselves?" Sam suggested.

The girls were greeted warmly, and the staff suggested a tour. Almost two hours later, the girls reappeared, and they just wouldn't stop talking. C.W., Violet, and Sam just smiled.

"Did you see those wards?" Patsy exclaimed. "There is no privacy. The patients see each other and see what nurses are doing to them."

"I know," Sara chimed in. "I saw staff draw blood, do a breathing treatment, and change a dressing. The odor was not acceptable on some units."

"I know. Did you see the young man with his leg in traction? The wounds were horrific. There were doctors and nurses everywhere. At least we will have resources for questions," Patsy shared.

"I am so excited. I am ready for this part of my life. I want to talk to everyone and soak up as much knowledge as I can. Dad, the secretary said they have all our paperwork. We are ready for the January semester," Sara said. She smiled from ear to ear.

"This is awesome. I will come to the farm for Christmas. Then, you will be here," C.W. said. "I'll make sure the flat is ready for you. Tonight, you can tell me what else you need, and I will have it delivered before January. I'll have the refrigerator stocked, too. We'll figure out what you need tonight."

"Well, I'm starving," Sam said. "I heard some nurses talking about the Wieners Circle in Lincoln Park, and they talked about poppy seed buns and a beef wiener with onions, dill pickle, and hot peppers. I want at least three." They all laughed and headed for Lincoln Park.

The hot dogs were delicious. C.W. announced, "I'm going to Michigan Avenue, and I have money for each of you to buy what you want. Nothing like a new pair of shoes, a hat, or a dress. What do you think, Violet? Something for you, too, Patsy. It will be fun."

"I always did like a big spender." Violet laughed.

Sara asked quietly, "Grandma, can we buy some Christmas presents here? I'd like to get Dad a nice jacket and C.W. something cool for his lifestyle. C.W. doesn't care how much we spend. He's a wealthy man."

"What a great idea, Sara. Let's see what we can find and then, since we only have a month before you come back to Chicago, we will have time to enjoy family."

"Good, because Sam and I are going to The Billy Goat Tavern on the corner of Michigan." The girls rolled their eyes. "We will meet right here in two hours and see if you're ready to go."

Everyone excitedly went their own way. Violet had a roll of money from C.W.

Sam hadn't been in a tavern for years. The women. Oh yes, the women. They all knew C.W. and wanted to know Sam. The flirting came from every direction and every woman. Unfortunately, or fortunately, Sam wasn't looking for this kind of woman. He played along—after all, you can do anything for two hours.

Sam told C.W., "We need to meet the girls. They'll be waiting on us."

"You're right. We need to go." The ladies reluctantly let them go, and Sam was relieved when they hit the doors. Sam and C.W. walked briskly down Michigan Ave. taking in the sights.

They finally got to the store where they'd left the girls and looked around. The girls were just coming out with more packages than they could hardly carry.

"Good grief, ladies, did you buy out the store?" Sam chuckled. As C.W. took some packages, he remarked, "I knew this was going to happen, and I'm glad you had fun. You can't get out of Chicago without more than a dozen bags full of goodies."

Sara had finished all her Christmas shopping. She'd gotten a shawl for Grandma and Pearline, as well as a small bottle of perfumed body lotion. Her favorite was a brooch with an amethyst in it for Grandma. C.W. got a leather jacket, and her father got a more traditional style. She'd bought a nice frame and intended to give Willis a picture of her to keep when she went to school. She'd also bought him a wool coat for when he came to Chicago to see her.

"I am so excited I have all my Christmas presents. It will be so much fun to wrap everything and put up the tree."

"Thank you for the new boots and sweater," Patsy said. "I love them both. Thanks for letting me come. We are going to have a great time here in Chicago."

"Isn't that the truth? I can't wait," Sara replied. In the same breath, Sara thought of Willis. The love of her life, and it might be months at a time of not seeing each other.

They made it home early Sunday after leaving Chicago at the crack of dawn. Sara called Willis the minute they got home and asked him over for supper.

She threw on her coat as she saw Willis pull in and met him before he could get out of the car. He immediately leaned down and kissed her. It was the warmth of his body against her that made her weak. For an instant Willis went very still, then he wrapped his arms around her, and she was on tiptoe crushed against him. "I love the way you kiss me, Sara."

She ran her hands over his back and shoulders and clasped them behind his neck, then raised her head and kissed him again. He felt a need for more, but they were in her driveway. When his mouth left hers and nuzzled her throat, she gasped for air. "We'd better head in, Willis."

"I know, Sara. I've missed you. We need to spend some time together and talk before you leave for school."

"We will. I promise. You can come see me as well. We can talk on the phone, and I'll come home when I can. This is all new territory for me, and I don't know how classes are scheduled."

The days passed quickly, and finally Patsy and Sara were in Chicago. They had loaded Sara's car with their belongings and hit the road. Although Sara had left a message for C.W., he wasn't to be found.

The girls unpacked. Sara placed her bras and panties in one drawer and her nightgowns in the next. The refrigerator and pantry were both stocked but in disarray. Sara stacked the corn together, then the green beans. Everything was organized. The pasta bags were laid one behind the other. "Much better."

"Let's go for a walk and get a quick bite," Sara suggested. After the long ride, they were ready to walk and explore. Patsy commented on all the men, and Sara, on the stores. Sara felt herself looking for C.W. They walked the neighborhood and down Michigan street again. They were in awe of all the new surroundings and could barely contain their excitement.

They finally settled for a burger and then went home to settle in before school began. Sara went to the bay window and wondered where C.W. was. He should be here to celebrate. After all, he'd gotten the house for her. She stared out the window watching traffic, wishing C.W. were there.

Classes started immediately, and there was hardly any personal time. They both went home and crashed until they started it all again the next day. Sara knew anatomy well from Grandma's training. Physiology was another story. She wanted to know more about how the systems worked together at the cellular level. Every day was something new. They did rotations through the different specialties. Medications were passed daily, and the wounds were astronomical. So many Sara had never seen before, but she quickly learned how to treat a burn versus a trauma wound.

Sara excelled. Learning Grandma's way had been easy, but now there were controlled ways to do everything in order to stay within the law and to meet regulations.

Dr. Martin met with Sara after only a month, inquiring about her skills.

"Sara, your documentation is excellent. I love reading your history and physicals, as you paint a picture that is excellent. If you are a first-year student, where did you learn this so quickly?"

"Thank you, Dr. Martin. I spent a lot of time doing house calls with my grandmother. She is a mid-wife and takes care of a lot of folks in our county. Dr. Gerstein taught me a lot, too. I have been going with Grandma since I was eight years old."

"Wow, that is amazing, Sara. Let's have lunch one day this week, and you can tell me all about it. I'll start teaching you more about physiology since you have the basics, and that will help you a lot."

"I'd love to go to lunch and talk. I have to run. I need to finish stocking the dressings in the supply closet."

In the following weeks, Sara learned more about infectious disease, sterilization, and infection control. It all made sense. She excelled with the doctors and would assist with every procedure she could. She rounded with them daily, hanging on every word they said. She then rotated throughout the specialties in the hospital. She soon realized conditions were not ideal. The wards promoted a lack of privacy. Odors were offensive, and there was a staffing shortage. Often, Sara spent the first hours of her day doing vital signs, passing trays, assisting with meals, and bathing. Sara could see it was free labor, but she was there to learn and took every opportunity she could.

After sixty straight days of shifts, Sara requested a few days off. Patsy was staying at the flat and working, as she seemed to be burning the midnight oil dating numerous men and working long hours. Sara wanted to see Willis and her dad and grandma. C.W. had called a couple of times, but she knew something was going on when he was absent. She wondered whether he was at the farm. She was going to surprise everyone.

Sara was getting ready to walk out the door and head for the farm when the doorbell rang. She ran to the door to see a courier standing there.

"Please sign here." The courier pointed.

Sara signed, took the package, and closed the door behind her. In the envelope were thousands of dollars from C.W. with a note. *"Wish I could get to the flat to see you, but too dangerous right now. Use this for whatever you need or want."* A beautiful pair of pearl earrings rested in the money with another note, saying, *"I love you."*

Now, Sara was worried, but she had to get to the farm. Maybe C.W. was already there.

It was mid-morning when Sara arrived at the farm. She saw her dad at the corncrib and started walking that way. When he saw her, he ran to meet her and hugged her as though she had been gone for a year.

"I missed you, Dad," Sara said. "I decided to take a few days and rest up."

"Good. It's too quiet around here. Grandma sure does miss you. She stays busy though. We haven't heard much from C.W. Have you seen him?"

"No. I was wondering if he was here for some crazy reason. I received a package from him right before I left. You know, money and pearl earrings. A girl's best friend." Sara laughed. "I'll look him up when I get back to Chicago. I'm going to go surprise Grandma and tell her all about school."

Violet had already spotted Sara and met her halfway. "Girl, look at you. You look beautiful. Tell me all about school." The talk was non-stop for the next two hours. Then, Sam came in, and she told him what she had been doing.

After lunch, the mail arrived with a large package for Sam and one for Violet. Sara said, "I bet it's from C.W. Open it." Both started opening their package. Sure enough, it was money.

"We're going to have to get a safe pretty soon, Dad. I know he has given us money for years. Don't quite know why you still farm and kill yourselves. We are far from poor," Sara said.

"You're right," Sam responded. "We are well prepared for anything. I want to work and show something for my work. I actually like farming most of the time. When the time comes, we will use the money for you or to help someone who needs help. Just like we always have. I may not give money away, but I get lumber and help neighbors and friends rebuild a barn that has burnt down. I will always do that. We are to help each other in life—and especially those less fortunate."

"I know, Dad. I just don't want you and Grandma to wear your-selves down and get sick."

"Honey, life is about working, family, and caring," Violet shared. "Your dad and I stay busy because we want to. Don't you worry."

"I'm going to Willis' for a while. I'll be back for supper."

"He has really been missing you," Violet said.

Sara saw Willis at the barn. She parked the car and walked to him. He was wearing a t-shirt, and she could see the hardness of his muscles beneath the shirt. As she walked closer, a wide smile spread across his face with such pleasure to see her. They went into each other's arms. She could feel the warmth of his breath and the pressure of his body against hers. His lips were cool as they touched, but seconds later, he kissed her hungrily with a heat they could not fight. Her breathing stopped. She felt weak. He lifted his head, and she looked into those dark eyes with a desire she wanted to complete. Their eyes were locked, their bodies touching, fierce heat between them. Willis leaned forward with a gentle kiss that barely brushed across her lips.

Willis smiled coyly. "Did you come looking for me?"

"I think I've been looking for you all my life." He was still as she brushed his lips with a kiss. He returned the kiss with a deeper kiss that made her weak and lightheaded.

"I love you, Willis," Sara whispered.

"I have loved you for the longest time. I want to spend my life with you." Willis sighed. They both saw Willis' dad driving in on the tractor. Sara waved. They talked about school a while, then his dad went back out to the field. Sara said she was thirsty and headed for the house. Willis looked at her long legs and cute tush as she walked away.

Sara returned with two teas. As Sara looked up at his hard, fa-miliar face, they stared at each other for the longest time. Then, he kissed her again with an explosion of passion they both wanted to explore. She couldn't control her physical response and curled her arms around him. His mouth left hers and slid down her neck, his hand covering her breast. She felt a gentle tremor, and her breathing stopped. Her heart was pounding, and her legs felt weak. Sara pressed her body into his.

The sound of the tractor was getting louder. They released each other and stepped into the open. They walked hand-in-hand to Sara's car. They both wanted more from each other.

"Willis, will you plan on coming to Chicago in a few months? I'll let you know when Patsy is going to be gone, and we can spend time by ourselves. Patsy is dating every Tom, Dick, and Harry in Chicago. I hope she can maintain her grades because she never studies anymore."

Willis chuckled.

"I will make plans to come see you. It will be a turning point for us. There will be no turning back. I love you so much."

"I know," Sara whispered. "I love you, too. Come to dinner tomorrow. We'll look at the house you and C.W. have been working on."

Sara returned to the farm where Sheba met her as she stopped the car. They had both missed each other. Sara sat on the step and drew Sheba close. "I wish I could take you with me, but it wouldn't be fair to you. You couldn't run and chase rabbits. Honking horns and noise all day long. I need you to understand this is your home. I am seldom at the house, and you would be alone most days. I won't be gone that long." She hugged Sheba tighter.

Sara returned to Chicago Sunday afternoon. No Patsy in sight. She returned in the middle of the night smelling of alcohol—a little too much alcohol. She staggered to her room and fell on the bed. The following morning, Sara was up early, fixed a scrambled egg, and looked in on Patsy. Sara tried to rouse her, but she only rolled over. Sara didn't want to be late, so she left for school.

Sara, you will be on medical surgical today," said Nurse Jensen.

"Yes, ma'am," Sara responded and headed for the wing. Dr. Oliver stopped her as she hit the floor. They rounded together and

110

changed orders on twelve patients. Next, she changed dressings for surgical and trauma patients.

Patsy showed up at noon, looking pretty rough. Sara didn't comment on her being late but observed her performance. Her attitude was negative, and she really didn't want to be working. It was obvious. Sara separated herself and continued with her assignment.

Later, as Sara parked in front of the flat, she saw C.W. walking towards her. She was thrilled.

"Quick, let's get inside." He practically pushed her in the door. Then, C.W. hugged her. "Things are escalating, Sara. A couple of the boys have been assaulted and beaten. The mob is trying to get information regarding a warehouse break-in. They have been looking for the thieves for three months now. I don't want them to follow me, so I was very cautious coming today. Are things going well at school?"

Sara responded quickly. "For me, yes. I am learning so much. Patsy is another story. She's drinking and not studying. I don't get it. She was so excited about being a nurse."

"I know. I saw her with a rough character a few days ago. I made sure she didn't see me. I'm worried," C.W. shared. "She doesn't know who she's dealing with. You haven't said anything about me and any details, have you?"

"Of course not. That will never come up. Is she hanging with the mob?"

"Yes, and others, too. Maybe you can talk to her tonight, if she comes home. She cannot be bringing mobsters here. It could be devastating for us. She can't take them next door either, so hide the key or keep it on you. Maybe tell her you rented the flat out. Reason being, if me or Sullivan or my closest boys needed help, this is a place I could keep them safely."

"I understand. I think she will be home tonight," Sara said. "She was hung over and tired. If she has any sense, she will come in early. I don't think she's going to listen to me, though. I think she's living for the moment. She's never been exposed to all that is here in Chicago."

"You're probably right," C.W. agreed. "The excitement has gotten hold of her. If you hear anything in the night, I may stay next door occasionally. Just lying low."

"Please don't get hurt, C.W. I don't have anything here to save you. I will be more than distraught."

"Gotta go. I'll see you soon. Remember, I will always love you." C.W. left quietly, leaving Sara with a foreboding.

It was three in the morning when the phone rang.

"Hello?" Sara said, as she fumbled for the phone.

"Sara, this is Mary in the emergency department at County. Can you come in? We have a mob war, and I need help. Sara's heart was pumping erratically, and she felt a lump in her throat.

"Yes, I'll get dressed and be there." Sara literally jumped in her clothes, raked a brush through her hair, and brushed her teeth. She smeared on some lipstick and ran for the door. Then, she stopped and went to see whether Patsy had come home. Her bed was empty.

She ran for the car. As Sara pulled into the hospital, she saw it was a flurry of activity. Police cars were squawking, lights flashing. As she walked to the emergency department, the police stopped her. "No one can pass this point. What's your business here," asked the officer.

"I'm a student here, and Mary asked me to come in. Said there was an accident. Can I get in to help, sir?" Sara asked.

"Yes, go on in," Sergeant Moreno barked.

Mary was right. It was total chaos. "What patient do you want me to start with?" Sara asked Mary.

"Room two. Get an intravenous solution going, hook them up to the monitor, and let me know the severity of that knife wound in his thigh," Mary said.

Sara took off. She grabbed the supplies she needed and did a complete assessment of the white male, approximately age forty. Pale in color, semi-comatose, and becoming short of breath. He could barely be aroused to respond. Visible wound, left thigh. Gross blood loss. Artery spurting. Sara grabbed the hemostats and started digging for the bleeder. She located it and clamped after several attempts. Sara quickly washed her hands. She lifted her patient's head and applied the oxygen mask. After cutting off his shirt, Sara started the intravenous fluids and had them wide open. She started cleaning up the blood to get a true picture of the wound. She irrigated the wound and disposed of the bloody linens.

Dr. Simpson walked in and saw the hemostats hanging on the artery. "Did you clamp that artery?"

"Yes, sir," responded Sara. "There wasn't anyone else to do it, and he was losing consciousness. He has a deep knife wound. I clamped the artery, have the fluids wide open, and oxygen. I just irrigated the wound. Shall I set up sterile field for suturing?"

"It looks like you have it under control. I imagine you could have sutured it, too, from the looks of everything. Am I right?" questioned Dr. Simpson.

"Well, yes, sir. I have sutured wounds before." Sara opened the sterile pack for Dr. Simpson and dropped the sterile suture on the field. "Do you want another type of suture for the surface or just this one will suffice?"

"Sara, this is good," Dr Simpson responded. "Let's see in a few minutes if I need more. Where did you suture before?"

"My grandmother is a midwife, and she taught me. Dr. Gerstein, in Southern Illinois, coached me on it as well. We take care of a lot of the people in the county. I know everyone, and you can't imagine what I have seen. Been doing it since I was eight."

"Well, you saved this man's life. He would have bled to death. I can see that when I took the hemostat off. You should stay in the emergency room, and you will learn a lot more. I'll recommend it to Mary."

"Thanks," Sara responded. "I need to go and see what else I can do to help. There's like twelve patients in the treatment rooms and the hallway. I'll be back."

Sara found Mary and helped her cut the clothes off a gunshot victim. The right shoulder was limp, open, and tissue was hanging. Sara again stopped the bleeders and applied a temporary dressing. She called for an x-ray of the shoulder. Then, surgery would be determined.

Triage went on for two more hours. Then, the basics were done. Initial treatment started on the patients, and she was ready to go to bed. The day staff was coming in. Sara reported to the oncoming nurse on all the patients, as she had treated most of them. Her nurse's notes were complete. She just had to get Penicillin from the pharmacy, for the patient in room four, before she could leave.

As she entered the pharmacy, she found Pete filling orders.

"Can I help you with anything? I just need Penicillin for the emergency department. Had lots of patients since 3 a.m. Hey, what's this box of expired dressings and solutions for?"

"Oh, that's for destruction. Those are past their expiration dates. I cleaned the shelves last week and haven't destroyed it yet," Pete shared.

"Is there a possibility I can have it for the animals on the farm? My dog Sheba got a bad injury after a fight she was in, and I have to change her dressing three times a day. I'm always treating the animals," Sara said, as she smiled at Pete.

"Well, I guess so. I've given them to the indigent clinic before. The animals sound like they could use it, too. Pull your car up close, and I'll load it for you when you get ready to leave."

"Thanks, Pete. I'll bring you a picture of Sheba. You'll see what a good cause you have contributed to." Sara took the medication back to the emergency department and got her car. As she pulled away from the pharmacy, she waved at Pete.

Sara half-carried and half-drug the heavy box of supplies to the second flat. She placed it in the closet and closed the door, then she sat on the couch for five minutes in prayer and gratitude for getting through the night. Now, she had the supplies if she would ever need them for C.W.

114

Sara awoke on the couch three hours later. She was exhausted and needed to get in her bed. As she entered her flat, Sara could see there was still no Patsy.

The following day, Patsy returned. Sara was relaxing in the living room. "Do you have time to talk?" Sara asked.

"Yes, but I have to work at 3 p.m. today," Patsy said. "I hear last night was a fiasco at county."

"I know," Sara responded. "I went in at 3 a.m. and helped with twelve patients in emergency. It was hopping. I learned and saw a lot. I think I would like to spend more time there. It's never the same issue. Are you doing okay, Patsy? Seems like you're burning a candle at both ends. How's your grades?"

"My grades are just okay. I met someone, a lot of someone's. But then I started seeing Jerry a lot. He doesn't think I need to be in school. He wants me to spend all my time with him. Unfortunately, now my eyes are open, and he probably says the same thing to a lot of girls. He got a little mean the other night when we were out in the bar. I saw him in a different light when a man stood up to him. I think Jerry could kill someone very easily."

"That doesn't sound good. You haven't brought him here, have you?" asked Sara.

"No, I wouldn't want to do that. I don't think I need to see him anymore. I don't want him coming here and creating any hell for us."

"Thank you. I would really appreciate it if you don't bring guys over. My focus is school, and I want solitude here. I just don't want to worry about someone being here while I'm gone. I almost forgot. I rented the second flat out this week. I need the money for school. Just keeping you in the loop."

"Sounds good. I don't blame you for renting it out. Maybe we'll meet them soon. I hope they're nice."

"Me, too," Sara said.

CHAPTER 20

Little did Sara realize all hell would break loose in the next two weeks. A dark sedan pulled up in front of Sara's Pub. One of C.W.'s boys was opening the tavern door when shots rang out. Little Pete dropped inside the door, one scream coming from him. Everyone in the pub hit the floor, but there were still casualties.

Sullivan screamed, "Everyone get down."

The hysteria and terror reached a crescendo quickly. Men were crawling to the bar to get a second layer of protection from the bullets spraying the front of the bar. Two of C.W.'s men were critically injured. Sammie was hit in the chest, the bullet passing through his body. He was dead instantly. Martin was leaving the card game when a bullet hit him in the neck. Blood pooled around him in seconds. Sullivan was wounded by one of the bullets hitting the front windows of the pub. He dropped instantly.

As C.W.'s sedan pulled to a stop in front of the pub, he rolled out of the door onto the pavement with guns drawn. As the attackers pulled away from the pub, C.W. got off several shots and knew one had hit its target.

The assailants were in a black Chevy, and he took down the license plate. There would now be a way to track down the assailants.

C.W. entered the pub from the side door and went down to the floor as he opened the hidden door behind the bar. Everyone was in a panic. "Don't shoot!" C.W. yelled. "I'm coming in."

Blood surrounded Martin like a silk blanket. Sullivan was down but breathing. He wasn't responding. C.W. called for the ambulance. When it arrived, the police did as well. The story was set.

Unknown assailants. They were all pinned down and saw nothing. There were no bystanders outside who saw or heard anything.

Sullivan was loaded onto the stretcher. Three other customers had minor injuries. Two of C.W.'s men were dead. C.W. stayed at the bar. One of the officers, Burton, was on C.W.'s payroll. He gave him the license plate number to run a check for the owner.

"What the hell happened here, C.W.?"

"Not sure. I believe it's the Chicago St. Louis gambling syndicate. I left some enemies when I left St. Louis. They never forget or forgive." C.W. sighed.

Burton replied, "I'll get this plate run and get back to you. In the meantime, stay on the alert. I'd keep a guard out after dark, if I were you."

Sara was in the emergency department again when Sullivan arrived. She was the best little actress in town. She didn't know him. "Mr. Sullivan, I'm going to remove your shirt and get the paperwork going." She was distraught not knowing where C.W. was.

Sara completed the paperwork and got intravenous fluids going. Sullivan had lost blood. There was a bullet that had gone in under his shoulder. Sara ordered an x-ray. As she was cleaning the wound, Dr. Patterson arrived and started probing. Sara placed a pressure dressing on the wound and got Sullivan to the x-ray department. When the technician took over in x-ray, Sara grabbed the phone and dialed the pub. C.W. answered.

"What in the hell is going on there? Are you okay?" Sara said in a panic.

"I'm okay, Sara. Is Sullivan with you?"

"Yes, I have him in x-ray. You're sure? You are really okay?"

"Yes, the St. Louis mob did this. The police are here. Just take care of Sullivan, and I'll pick him up if you don't admit him—or he won't stay, is more like it," C.W. said.

"Okay, I have to get back to work."

Sara went to check on Sullivan. "Sullivan, I just spoke with C.W. He has everything under control and will be here to check on you later. You need to be admitted." Sullivan just looked at Sara.

Burton returned to the pub that afternoon. "The car belongs to Garrison with the Chicago Mob. They're on the east side most days. Just be aware, he has a bodyguard now. So, don't go over there thinking he is alone. I'll be patrolling around the pub, and several of the guys are keeping their ear to the ground. I'll let you know what we hear—if anything." As C.W. shook with Burton, Burton became a few hundred richer.

C.W. went to county hospital to check on Sullivan. He had been right—Sullivan wasn't about to stay.

"I can't protect myself. I don't have a gun. This is like being at a turkey shoot, and I'm the turkey." Sullivan was doing his best to get his shirt on. Sara came in shaking her head.

"What are you doing, and where are you going?" Sara asked. "You have to have an intravenous antibiotic daily for seven days and a dressing change daily on your shoulder. You will have to have therapy so your shoulder doesn't freeze up."

C.W. laughed. "Honey, I told you he wouldn't stay. We'll hang out in the other flat, and you can take care of him for seven days. Then, he'll be good to go. I'll take him to therapy if I need to. Okay?"

"It's not okay, but I can't stop you." Sara smiled. "I'll get the doctor to get the paperwork ready for release. You're both crazy. You'll probably have to sign out against medical advice. I doubt the doctor will release you." Sara started toward the door. She was operating on a minimum of sleep. The dark circles under her eyes said it all.

"Yes, we are crazy," C.W. said.

Sullivan just chuckled, then winced in pain.

The police were doing a thorough investigation into all the shootings occurring in Chicago. About all they came up with were dirty cops. Now, it was a different investigation into shakedowns, kickbacks, and padded payrolls. They weren't able to find one person to indict in the shooting.

C.W. was leaning more toward getting out of this business. He had plenty of money. If he lived at the farm, he could live the simple life. It was time.

C.W. got Sullivan settled in at the flat. He wasn't staying. He felt he needed to be at the bar. Guards were posted outside in the shadows and on the roof. No more surprises.

In the meantime, C.W. was going to liquidate his holdings in Chicago. First, he had to get rid of the whiskey from the heist. It was in the warehouse he wanted to unload. This could be tricky. It would be open season on the Chicago Mob. He started a rumor that Garrison had taken the whiskey from the docks. Two weeks later, Garrison was hit in his right arm when he was driving to his home. The police said the gunfire had to come from a roof given the way the bullet had entered his arm.

Another two weeks after that, Garrison was at a local gas station when gunfire erupted. The assailants had followed him and were across the street in heavy undergrowth. At the first burst of gunfire, Garrison made it into the garage. He tried to escape out the back of the gas station and was cut down immediately in the back. He died in minutes.

Now, C.W. had to get rid of the liquor. He put the word out that he had bought liquor from Garrison, and he wanted to unload it because of its critical nature. It seemed a stretch to blame Garrison for the heist, but it worked. One thing seemed clear. Garrison's murder was a definite confirmation of his involvement in the whiskey heist.

The trucks and the booze had a price tag. It was non-negotiable. The highest bidder was the same mob he'd heisted it from originally. The warehouse was off limits. C.W. had the liquor and arms loaded on trucks from the mob. After receiving his hefty payment, the liquor was delivered to the docks. No one was the wiser.

C.W. went to the flat to check on Sullivan and Sara. He found Sara there, actively changing the dressing and doing range-of-motion exercises on Sullivan's shoulder and arm. She got up and hugged him.

"Good to see you, C.W. What's going on out there in your mishappen world?"

"I'm just setting the scene to accomplish what I need," C.W. said, laughing.

"What does that mean?" Sullivan asked, grinning from ear to ear.

"Well, I'm selling everything. I had to get rid of the evidence from the liquor heist and sold it back to the same mob I stole it from." They were both laughing.

"How did you do that?" Sullivan asked.

"I made it look like Garrison was responsible for it. After all, he's dead and can't talk," C.W. stated.

"Sara, I'm getting out of this business. Sullivan, you need to decide what you want to do. I'm going to farm, and you are welcome to join me. I'm going to buy some land and settle in closer to Sara."

Sara threw her arms around his neck. "REALLY? Are you positive?"

"Yes, I sold the liquor and trucks. Now, I will sell the warehouse and the guns. Then, I have to sell the bar, or Sullivan, you can buy it, and I will have a holding in it. What do you think?"

Sullivan laughed. "Well, you caught me at a bad time. Being shot and all. I think it's time to do something else, too. I've made a lot of money working with you. I have enough for a lifetime. You have enough for ten lifetimes, C.W. It is time to move on. We'll talk about what you have planned. I'm a damn good mechanic. I can fix anything."

"That's awesome. There will be a lot of machinery to keep running. After you're better, we'll look at everything available surrounding Sam's property," C.W. said, as he looked at Sara. Sara is probably getting married, and I want to be around. Maybe I'll see some babies and can be a part of their life."

"Oh, C.W., that's wonderful. I can't wait to tell Dad and Grandma. It will be great to have you there all the time."

Later, C.W. pulled Sara aside to talk with her.

"I wanted to run something by you, Sara. I am considering buying the Medlar property. It's in foreclosure and has been for years. Johnny and his dad were just squatting there. I feel I can clear the land. Make sure everything is settled in regards to Johnny's killings. I guess it would be putting closure on everything. You need closure, too, Sara."

"Yes, I do. Do you think we could build a huge complex there and have people who want to work for us live there? I would like it to represent a Spanish villa. It has to have a courtyard surrounding the homes, with a large fountain. Also, let's make a covered patio outside each door for families to enjoy the evenings with each other. It should have a brick oven and grill. That way everyone can eat together as a family. We can hire a cook. Or, maybe those who have lost everything at Johnny's hand can live there and find themselves again.

"I need to bring Mary there. Burt killed her husband, and she is wasting away. We haven't found the body, but I know it's on the property somewhere. I want to be present when the land is cleared. I know there was a lot of death there. Is that okay with you?"

"Absolutely, Sara. I know you are right, but slow down, girl. You're making my head spin. Everything you said is perfect. We can help others recover and give them a purpose in life. I have thought about this a lot the last three months. One thing you must know. I'm not leaving here until you graduate."

"Oh, you must love me, C.W." Sara smiled.

"That's right, smartass," C.W. joked.

"Wow, Sara. You and C.W. have this all planned out. I would love to be a part of it," Sullivan shared.

"I have another semester. That will give you plenty of time to sell everything. *If* it sells quickly, you can live here in this flat until I graduate. I think Patsy will flunk out soon," Sara said. She began writing in her planner. She had a lot to do.

The phone was ringing off the hook. Sara ran up the steps and unlocked the door. She barely got to the phone on the last ring.

"Sara, it's Patsy."

"Hi! How are you?"

"Well, I wanted to tell you the truth about my leaving. I know I was distant and didn't want to go to school," Patsy said quietly.

"Okay, Patsy. Tell me about it."

"I found out I was pregnant a few weeks ago, and it changed everything. It's Jerry's baby. He offered to pay to get rid of it, but I'm not sure I want to. I'm working through everything. He also asked me to go to Chicago. He'd get me a place and come see me. I'm not sure I want that life. It could get dangerous. I've seen what they do. It's hard for me right now because I can't make my mind up, and I am worried sick. I'm running out of time to make the right decision," Patsy said, as her voice cracked.

"I'm sorry, Patsy. I had no idea. You always told me you wanted babies. When you left, you said Jerry was rough with you. You didn't like it. Now, get a piece of paper and write pros on one side and cons on the other for both issues. First, the baby, and second, Jerry. I think you will see a bigger picture when you do that.

"Patsy, you have to look ahead. The past is gone. Now, a baby changes everything. In your heart, do you want it? I would pray to God to help me make the right decision. I don't think you want to be in an abusive relationship without true love. I will pray for you also. You will make the right decision. I have faith in you, and God will direct you to the decision that is His will. Call me after you do the pros and cons, and let's talk again. Don't forget. You can talk to Grandma, too. She loves you."

"I know. I may go see Violet. I'll be in touch."

CHAPTER 21

Six months after Sullivan's shooting, there was a closure to the Chicago life that was unexpected. In the wee hours of the morning, Sarah's Pub had gone up in flames. There was no liquor in the pub. C.W. had sold everything in the pub to Walker from his St. Louis days. He was just starting out in a new bar. C.W. told him he was remodeling the pub, and everything needed to go. There were a few suspicious looks from investigators, but in the end, the insurance paid out. The two henchmen sleeping in the bar were unscathed. When C.W. and Sullivan pulled up in front of the bar, Sullivan turned to C.W. and said, "Is this your idea of closure?"

"No one can own this bar. The land is for sale now. It was all about getting money to care for Sara. I don't even need money. I am filthy rich. I have given money to Sara and her family for years. They don't use it for themselves. They use it when the neighbors need something. I won't lie. It was exciting and kept my adrenalin going. I lived for the booze, the games, the fights, and the women. But I don't want any further history on it. This is closure to this life and a new beginning in life with Sara close by. I want a family I can see every day and truly live life with them by my side. It's hard to comprehend me saying this, isn't it, Sullivan?"

"I get it, C.W. I have the same desire after all these years for a simple life doing something I like. Maybe helping someone else for a change, is the key to happiness. I have only thought about myself for way too long. This will be another great venture with you. At least this one will be legal," Sullivan said, as they both started laughing.

"I have already moved all your belongings to the flat, as well as my own. We didn't lose a thing in the fire," C.W. said, smiling. "We will stay at the flat until after Sara's graduation. Then, we will sell the flat. I'm going to go ahead and buy the Medlar land. You and I will not have to worry about money ever again.

"Sara's dad and I go way back. I would like for the three of us to become the biggest farmers in the state. I intend to help the poor. That's what Sam and Violet have always done. When we get the living arrangements made for the workers and the victims of Johnny and Bart, I foresee another family emerging. Time will tell," C.W. said.

The last semester flew by. C.W. spent more time with Sara. "I didn't know you could cook so darn well. After all, you did learn from Violet. Dinner was delicious. Thank you, Sara. You don't have to cook for us. We can go out and eat whenever you want," C.W. said.

Sullivan said, "I haven't had meals this good most of my life, Sara. I want you to know I appreciate being here for each meal. Most of all, I appreciate you helping me get well."

"Let's go for a walk in the neighborhood and stop at the park and watch the ducks," Sara said. "I miss the animals. I'll get some bread to feed the ducks." The boys looked at each other, but they got up for the journey. It was a friendly walk, greeting other families along the way. C.W. and Sullivan both knew this was the life they would be involved in after a few more weeks. It was wholesome—something neither of them knew much about, but they liked it.

Sara graduated, and Violet and Sam shared that weekend with pride. As Sara walked across the stage for her diploma, they all recognized a smart young woman emerging. She was no longer a child, even though she would always be their baby.

Sullivan and C.W. were with them the entire time. Confidentially, C.W. shared the events surrounding the pub. Sam smiled. "I knew you would come around some day. I just thought I would be dead and gone." They all laughed. "C. W. what are your plans? Do you have any."

Sara, C.W., and Sullivan looked at each other and smiled. "Boy, do we have plans," Sara said. "C.W., why don't you and Sullivan give them the news?"

C.W. stated, "I have left the gangster life."

Sullivan perked up and said, "I have quit that life also. We are going to farm close to you, Sam."

"WHAT?" both Violet and Sam said at the same time in disbelief.

Sullivan continued. "We now own the Medlar property. We're going to take it apart inch by inch and discover the real story behind Johnny and Bart."

Violet and Sam's mouths dropped open. They were speechless.

"I want to be a part of this removal of debris, clearing the land, and finding who was buried there," Sara stated. "I want closure. I don't want the kudzu to remain. I want to know everything growing under it, why it's there, and whose lives it affected. I'm going to make everything they did as a crime right for the victims and their families."

Violet got up and hugged Sara.

C.W. shared, "We are going to farm the land. We will build a hacienda-style housing for workers and victims. It will have a courtyard for cooking and a place to eat outside together. Sullivan and I might live there temporarily. We are going to help others with the crops, the food, and be a good neighbor in general. Just like you, Sam. You and Violet have given to others all your lives."

126

Sullivan chimed in. "We are hoping to have vegetable stands and even sell jellies and canned goods, with your help, Violet. We'll also have others canning, but you are the expert."

"Wow, you all have been busy," Violet said. "I would love to do just that. I can teach others, and eventually they can support themselves. Things are sure changing quickly. I couldn't be more blessed knowing you will share our lives every day without fear. We are truly blessed with this change of heart. I know God will bless everything you do."

Sam looked around. "I think I missed a lot these last few months. Thank God you're all coming home, and I won't miss a thing."

Violet laughed. "That's for sure. I have a lot to do. This visit to Chicago has been a true blessing. I am so excited for all of you. I can't wait to have everyone settled in. You can all stay at our place or the old farm until you have everything built. This is going to be a very busy year."

The following week was busy. Violet and Sam left for the farm in the wee hours of the morning. They took as much as they could from the apartments. C.W. and Sullivan closed on the Medlar farm. Then, Sullivan listed the two-flat for sale.

Sara started packing her belongings. She looked at the furniture in both flats and went to find C.W. "Can we take all the furniture for the farmhouse and the apartments? I think we should. We'll be able to use it."

"Ah, so you liked what I picked out?" C.W. was baiting her.

"Well, it's not exactly farm or ranch style. Yes, I do like the more contemporary look. And don't try to snow me. I know Sullivan picked out the furniture." Sara slapped at C.W. playfully. "I'm sure it will be used by many over the years, and yes, there are a couple of pieces I want. There, I said it. You both have good taste. Satisfied?" Sara laughed, and C.W. joined in the laughter.

Sara continued to pack. C.W. hired a moving van that could do most of the heavy work, and the house was empty once again. The flat sold within two weeks. Chicago was a thing of the past.

CHAPTER 22

Sara drove her car home and went straight to Willis' farm. Willis was on his stallion when she pulled in. He started dismounting the moment he saw her car. His eyes were full of love. He watched her with appreciation for her beauty as she stepped from the car and walked to him.

Sara's heart was thundering and her blood, racing. She had grown up while in Chicago and matured physically. Sara looked at Willis' physique and admired his power when he walked to her. He put his arms around her and lifted her off the ground. His lips brushed her forehead. He tilted her chin and their eyes met. His body was emanating heat. Sara could hear her heartbeat as well. His mouth covered hers. She melted against him. They had a deep, all-consuming passion for each other.

Willis' brother arrived at the most inopportune time. Sara turned and said hello, but she kept a tight grip on Willis. She rested her head on his chest as they stood there wanting everything of each other and more.

"Willis, Dad needs you to bring the wagon down. He's removing a stump from the field," Bob conveyed, as he walked to the tractor.

"Be right down. Give us a moment, Sara just got home." The surroundings didn't matter. Once again, Willis kissed her, his tongue creating fire in her very being.

"That's probably the best way I have ever been greeted when I have come home. Could we do that again real soon?" Sara asked, chuckling.

"Let's go to a movie Saturday night. I don't think we will ever be alone between my family and yours," Willis stated.

"Well, you're right there, because C.W. and his best friend Sullivan have come here to live. They bought the Medlar farm and are going to clear it. They are staying at Grandma's house. They're going to continue remodeling it and get it ready to live in.

"I love you and have missed you," Sara added, smiling.

"I love you, Sara," Willis replied. He squeezed her hand and turned to get the wagon.

Sara came in the back door and found her grandma. "Patsy got pregnant, Grandma. She's really struggling. I told her everything that was an option. I feel sad, but she did want a baby. She mentioned an abortion. The dad is a mobster. C.W. told me he saw them and said he was a brute. I told her to pray about it."

"You did the right thing. Listen, but give her options. Prayer is the answer, and she will make the right decision," Violet said.

"I've been with Willis my whole life. I just saw him. We are both grown and have goals. It's different now, and we are both ready to start a life together. He's coming over tomorrow, and we're going to talk about what he expects, too. Grandma, I'm confused. I love Willis, but I want to see the world. I want to do all the things I read about in Pearline's books, and I want to travel everywhere I read about. Is that wrong? I may not be ready to be a wife, stay on the farm, and have babies. I see the world as an enormous opportunity to do anything I want."

"I understand," Violet responded. "You desire adventure. Just make sure Willis is on board with that. I'm sure he has thoughts on this as well. Somehow, you have to meet in the middle, if you are staying committed to each other. You have a lot of opportunity being a nurse. Yes, you can travel. How long would you be gone? Would you move? Where is Willis in this plan?"

"Oh Grandma, he's in the plan. I just don't know about marriage yet. He keeps bringing it up. I have a lot of soul searching to do."

Sara headed for Lover's Lane to think.

CHAPTER 23

The time spent at the kitchen table was the best. Everyone shared what was happening with them personally and what they were doing for the day. Sara was beaming when she sat down for lunch. Everyone could tell she was ecstatic with news to share. Finally, C.W. and Sullivan arrived. After they washed up, they sat down. Immediately, Sara said, "I got a part-time job at the hospital in the emergency department and a day in home health here in this county. It's all through the hospital. I didn't want to work full time right now because I want to help clear the land on your new property, C.W."

"Congratulations, Sara," Sullivan said.

Then, C.W. shouted, "Awesome. I knew you would get the job you wanted. I heard you tell Violet, over a year ago, you were coming back to take care of the neighbors here in your county. I'm proud of you."

Sam smiled. "That's great news. I'm also glad to hear you call it C.W.'s property and not Medlar's place. That is over and done. We are clearing the field today that surrounds the house."

"I'll bring the machete and start clearing closest to the old house," Sara said.

Willis arrived and sat down with them.

"Sara, I'll help you clear the kudzu," he said. "It's pretty thick, and it will take two of us." Violet offered him a plate, and he thanked her. He loved having Sara home, and this week they were working on the land—but doing it together.

"We're going to test the soil today in various places. Fertilizing and prepping the soil is the priority. It's nice having several of us doing this. Everything goes faster. Of course, I'm no expert, so Sam, you can chime in anytime. I need all the help I can get," C.W. said.

Sam laughed. "Well, we'll start with plowing and clearing the old vegetation, weeds, bushes, and debris. Then, we can see if you need any fences. I recommend you leave a row of trees for shade along the creek bed that runs through the property. That's in case you want any horses or cattle. We can figure that out later."

C.W. looked at Sullivan. "The job just got bigger than what I imagined." They all laughed. "Let's get some gloves for everyone. Willis, you and Sara can take the smaller tools in the truck. We'll be taking the tractors. I'm going to purchase a couple of tractors next week. Sam, what do you recommend?"

"Let's look at what we really need for you to be successful," Sam responded. "We'll make a list. Sounds like you want a garden, too. What about chickens? This is all a process and a plan, C.W. We'll sit down with you and Sullivan and determine how big this production is going to be. Finally, we can set timelines. See, you're going to have to build barns to house the equipment. Corncribs are necessary. Chicken houses and much more. Today, let's just get out there and clear land."

Everyone headed for the door.

Sara and Willis loaded the truck with shovels, picks, and rakes. "Grab me a pair of gloves?" Willis asked.

She tried on two pairs for her smaller hands. "It seems so strange pulling in here. I don't feel scared anymore. I just want this to all go away."

"It will, Sara." Willis parked the truck close to the gate. "This is where you want to start, isn't it?" Willis asked.

133

"This is good. I want to work my way to the back of the property and not miss anything," Sara said.

The kudzu turned out to be tedious work. Willis was working on most of the root system, while Sara clipped and piled the vines and branches into a burn pile. Eventually, old items from days gone by were unveiled from the cloak of the kudzu. "Willis," Sara called out urgently. "Look at the bicycle. I wonder if this was Johnny's."

Willis moved the bicycle to another pile. He then worked closer with Sara to remove trash that was being revealed as they cut the vines. Next came parts of a grist mill. "I bet C.W. can do something with this," Sara said. "Maybe just a decoration. It's definitely not going anywhere. It weighs a ton."

As they continued to clear, more parts to the grist mill were discovered. They piled them together. An old watering can as well as a wrench were the next treasures. They kept cutting. Broken flower-pots were put in the trash pile, along with a rusting wringer washer. Sara's back was already aching from working in a bent over position. She straightened. "Willis, let's take a break for a few minutes."

"Gladly. This is a killer with all the bending and cutting. I'll probably have to crawl home," Willis said, groaning. "Let's walk around and see what else is here."

Willis took Sara's hand and gave her a hug. When they got to the wooded area, the ground had been broken, and they saw a pile of dirt that looked suspicious.

"No, we're not digging this up. In my soul, I know there are bodies here. That is the last thing I want to do on this property. I want to uncover everything else first," Sara stated.

"I understand," Willis said quietly. "I know this is a project for you, Sara. It's a way to get closure, and then you will never look back. I get it. You have been through a lot related to this property and the people who lived here."

Sara turned on her heel and headed back to the kudzu project. They worked until dark, and then they all headed for the house.

The best thing about the day was knowing Violet had a great meal waiting for them.

They all bathed before eating. Willis had to leave and feed the animals. C.W. and Sullivan cleaned up in the old farmhouse, and Sara bathed quickly, while Sam bathed in the outdoor shower behind the garage. As they gathered at the table, they all hugged Violet.

"Grandma, I am so tired I can hardly walk. I'm not used to this type of work. It's a killer," Sara shared.

C.W. laughed. "You are a wussy."

"Well now, C.W., I heard you doing a little bit of grumbling today, too," Sullivan said.

"Hush now, you're supposed to keep quiet." C.W. laughed. "I can see where this is going. You're ganging up on me."

"C.W., I don't have the energy to gang up on you. But I will at another time. I'm watching you," Sara declared. "We found a grist mill today. Maybe you can make something out of it as a decoration for the courtyard. If we could run water to it like a waterfall, it would be a great piece."

"What's this *we* stuff." C.W. laughed. "You got a mouse in your pocket?"

"Hahaha," Sara came back at him. "I just know what will look good."

"Okay, we'll do it," C.W. declared.

Sam laughed. "Good thing you gave in. I guarantee you won't win. I'm going to bed. These last weeks have kicked my butt."

Everyone agreed and headed to bed. Sara stayed and helped Violet clear the table and clean up. They hadn't had much time together.

"We have made a lot of progress on the land, but I'm not used to this kind of labor, Grandma," Sara said again.

"Of course you're not. But I think when it's done, you will have achieved a lot. It's a great project to help others start over. I am so proud of you, C.W., and Sullivan. Great things will come out of this."

"I wish I could help you more, but I am so focused on the land, I stay there until dark."

"Don't worry about it. I'm fine. The work is steady in the house. Get to bed. Kitchen is clean. Love you. Goodnight."

"Night, Grandma."

They started early the next day. Everyone was helping Sara clear kudzu. Willis had to help his dad farm all week.

Sara uncovered an antique well pump and was trying to dislodge it from the vines. "Look, C.W. Here's another piece for the courtyard. We can plant flowers around it."

"C.W. learned quickly. "Yes, ma'am, we sure can use it." Sam and Sullivan slapped their legs in unison and laughed at him.

CHAPTER 24

The weeks passed quickly. There was still a section of kudzu to clear. Old glass bottles were lying in the kudzu, and Sara retrieved them all. She carried broken wooden furniture to the burn pile. Sullivan left to clear the fields, while Sam and C.W. tore at the kudzu jungle. C.W. and Sam went to the barn for a short break.

"What should we build and where? There isn't one standing structure worth salvaging," C.W. said.

"You're right. We'll start from scratch after we tear everything down. You have to make it functional. You don't want the chicken house close to where the tractor is. They'll be scared, and you'll always have to watch out for them. It needs to be closer to the house. The barn needs to have a corncrib and a cover for the machinery. So, you have to decide how much equipment you want to have. Next, do you want horses or cows now or later? You don't have to have them. They do require a lot more work and feeding. We have to decide where you will build the housing for the workers and the houses for you and Sullivan. You both may end up meeting a woman and getting married," Sam added.

"Wouldn't that be something. I think I would enjoy settling down. I'm still young enough to have kids. Oh hell. If it's to happen, it will. I have so much work here, I'll be old and gray before it's the way we want it," C.W. said. "If you'll walk the land with me and Sullivan this week, I think we need to go ahead and decide where the houses will be."

"Be glad to. Let's get back to work."

They carried a couple of rotted boards from the barn to the burn pile. Then they entered the old house, picked up broken furniture, and returned to the burn pile repeatedly. There hadn't been that much in the house anyway in the way of furniture.

The windows were broken out. Sam pulled out the window frame, and coins rolled to the floor. C.W. walked over and they looked in the windowsill. It was full of silver dollars. Sam put his hand up for C.W. to stop.

"Bart's wife told Violet that Bart had killed Mary's husband one night in a drunken rage. He had a silver dollar collection, and Mary said she doesn't know where it is. We will need to return all this to Mary. Go get Sara. I want her to see this and know she will need to look under everything."

C.W. went to get Sara.

"Oh my! Dad, is this Mary's coin collection?" asked Sara when she came in.

"I think so. She is getting forgetful, but I think we need to give everything in this windowsill to her. Let's find a container and pull it out now. We'll take it to the farm and have her over for dinner Sunday. We'll give it to her then."

C.W. was in full agreement. The demolishment of the house continued.

"We're going to have to burn today, the pile is getting too big. I don't want it out of control," C.W. stated.

"I agree," Sam said. "You start the fire. Are there any water sources here? If not, let's dig a trench around the pile. It's pretty big already."

They started trenching around the pile. The fire was roaring in no time. Sam and C.W. started on the few walls. "Let's pull down the remaining roof and walls with the tractor. Then, we just carry it to the burn pile."

"Okay. Let me get the tractor and chain."

C.W. returned on the tractor. They secured the chain around a corner stud, and the rotten house was soon history. Sara stood and watched it go. They had moved the still to protect it. She helped carry the studs to the fire. It was huge. Sara picked up a crowbar to pull up the flooring. Below the first board was a metal box. It held stacks of hundred-dollar bills. Who would have thought?

"Dad! Come quick."

C.W. and Sam came running and just stared. Sam shook his head. "Why would a man let his family live in squalor his whole life and have money for heat and water all along? They didn't have food most of the time. I let them take corn for nothing, and they stole from the garden. I didn't care until they wanted to hurt us."

"Dad, I think it had to do with Bart's mental neglect and deterioration from whiskey. There are thousands of dollars here. Johnny started having more of the same symptoms the last few years. Sadly, their past is such an enigma. Unfortunately, I know we are going to reveal more over the months to come."

Everyone was quiet. Finally, Sara said, "Let's take this to the farm, and we will give it to someone who comes to live and work for us that is having hard times. Or we can use it to get the farm started."

The men, still quiet, just nodded their heads in agreement.

"Let's pull the rest of the floor up," Sara said. "Then, as soon as the fire is low, I'm ready to call it a day."

The first thing they all did when they quit working was to bathe. Then they were ready for dinner. Sam and C.W. carried in the coins and metal box.

They shared with Violet their treasure. "Oh Sam, I think that is Mary's silver dollar collection. We'll never know if her husband bought whiskey with it or what the truth is."

"Let's have her over for Sunday dinner. We'll pick her up, and then we'll present it to her," Sam offered.

Violet was teary-eyed. There was good coming out of so much bad.

"Look at this metal box from the floorboards. It's full of money. We don't know anything about it, so we're going to put it to good use when the time comes," Sara said.

Violet was in awe.

"C.W., it sure is exciting having you and Sullivan around. Never a dull moment," Violet declared, as she smiled at them both. "Let's eat."

Sara said the prayer. "Our Father in Heaven, we thank you for allowing C.W. and Sullivan to rectify their lives. We pray for forgiveness of our sins. Thank You for letting us be physically able to clear the land and help others with the treasures found. I pray for Your guardian angels around us, and we will do Your will. Thank You for the food prepared. Praise God. Amen."

You could have heard a pin drop. The prayer touched them all.

Following dinner, they went to the front porch and shared the day and their plans. Mostly C.W.'s and Sullivan's.

Sam said, "Why don't you keep the housing for the workers exactly where Medlar's place is? C.W., you could take the acreage to the west to build on. This would put you close to Pearline's place, and she needs more help now that she is older. Sullivan, you could take the property to the east of Medlar's place and build. Both of you can come up with where you want the house, the barn, and whatever else you want to build. This way the workers have access to both of you if needed."

They nodded and continued to discuss options.

"We're going to have to work our farm the next two days," Sam said. "Violet is handling our clothes, the meals, cleaning, and the garden. Let's stay home a few days and help her."

"Gladly," Sara said, "but I have a shift at the hospital."

They all agreed on a short break, each welcoming the chance to catch up on their own obligations. The weekend was a flurry of activity. Mary, Willis, and Pearline came for Sunday dinner.

"Mary, we have a surprise for you," Sam said. "We've been demolishing the Medlar house, and your silver dollar collection was found." He stood up, retrieved the coins, and set them beside her. She picked up a few coins, speechless.

"I never thought I would see this again," Mary stated. She became emotional and excused herself. Violet left the table to console her. They returned after a few minutes.

"Thank you for doing this. I can never repay you. At this time, can I ask you to keep the collection here? The house is in horrible condition and not very safe for valuables. You have helped me more than you will ever know."

"Of course we will. Violet can be in charge of keeping the collection for you. We also wanted to ask if you would want to move to the new housing we are building on Medlar's place. C.W. owns it now. We're going to start canning and sell more than we have in the past. We'll have a huge garden and sell vegetables, too. Pearline, you are welcome to help with our new business, too. I know you are both experts."

Pearline looked at Mary. "If you want to live with me until the housing is finished, I would love to have the company. We can plan on what to can and how much. We can determine what supplies we need, since it will be a larger quantity."

"I am so blessed today," Mary said quietly. "I would love to move to your house, Pearline, if you really don't mind. I don't have much to bring with me. Thank you again, Sam, for returning my coins."

"They were yours to begin with. We're honored to return it." Sam patted Mary's hand kindly. "Now, Pearline, we have the money from your Social Security check that Johnny took. It was under the floorboards."

He extended the money to Pearline, and she took it. Her hands went to her chest. "I never thought I would see it again. Thank you so much."

The chatter continued regarding the new houses for Sullivan and C.W. Pearline was thrilled to have a neighbor closer.

CHAPTER 25

The following week had to be devoted to farming. Sara insisted she would continue removing kudzu. Four hours into the day, Sara revealed the back of a Chevrolet Belair. She continued until she had one side released from the kudzu.

"Wow, this is a cool car. The boys will like this," Sara said out loud. She moved to clear the opposite side of the car. She knew it was time for lunch but ignored her stomach. She wanted to get in the car, so she worked through lunch knowing someone would probably come check on her. They would be worrying about why she hadn't shown up.

Sara opened the back of the car to find a skeleton of a child lying flat in the back seat. She couldn't breathe. She backed away, gasping, then slid to the ground trying to get a grip on herself. Sara took her gun out of the holster and shot twice.

Everyone at the table stood so quickly when the shots rang out, the chairs fell to the floor. They were all racing for the car. "This is bad," Sam said. C.W. was white as a ghost, and Sullivan had already gotten to the car and started it.

"I shouldn't have left her alone," C.W. said.

God help anyone on that short road to Sara. They were careening down the driveway. Sam slid across the back seat when they turned onto the gravel road without looking or stopping. They tore into the lane and found Sara. She was sitting beside the car. They all jumped out of the car and ran to Sara.

"Are you hurt? What's wrong?" Sam yelled.

"Look in the back seat," Sara whispered. "There's a hand coming through the seat from the trunk. I need you to open the trunk. Sara got up and moved so she could see. They all stared at the child and were saddened. They looked in the ignition and took the key.

"Don't touch anything in the car. We have to call Sheriff Bone after we pop this trunk."

A sudden bolt of fear went through Sara. Her heart was pounding. The skeletal remains were all that was left—the hand extending through the back seat to the child most likely for comfort. Sara sobbed. "How could anyone do this?" she said. Her hands were shaking. She took a deep breath, then looked at the murder scene one last time.

"Stay with her, C.W. I have to get the sheriff out here." Sam hugged Sara. "I'm so sorry," he said. He drove to the house and told Violet the gory details. Violet turned off the stove. She walked through the field to comfort Sara. She saw C.W. holding Sara as she drew close. Violet walked to the car and peered in both the trunk and the back seat. Then, Violet put her arms around Sara and drew her away from the site.

"I remember a girl and child from Mount Vernon went missing at least a year ago. I would put my money on it being her. This is truly closure on a life that has devastated many people's existence. This will not be the only body we find."

"Grandma, this could have been me. Johnny was mentally ill. I am so saddened by this baby and her mother. I know you're right about more bodies to be found. I have to do something for the families. I just don't know what just yet. I'll wait to see how many more."

Sheriff Bone arrived. "Sam, we really have to stop meeting this way. You are the most excitement in my career. Everything else is traffic tickets and domestic violence."

Sheriff Bone went straight to the bodies and shook his head. "Why are you on this property?" Sheriff Bone asked.

"My friends just bought this property," Sam said. "It was in foreclosure, and I promised to help them clear it. They want to farm it. We have been helping clear it. It helps with closure after what Johnny has done to everyone over the years. Sara was helping, too."

"Based on my knowledge of Johnny and Bart, and the unknown cause of death of two victims, these are circumstances that indicate a suspicious death," stated Bone. "I know the death wasn't natural. Were they alive when placed in the car? Most likely, yes. The coroner may determine the death was from blunt trauma or something else. I'm sure the coroner will consider this an unattended death, and a post-mortem autopsy will be done. We have to find their identities, if possible. I'll check the glovebox for ownership papers. Was there a purse on the body in the trunk?"

The Medical Examiner arrived. The crime scene was taped off. Bone called in the State Police for assistance after sharing the details they had discovered, then Bone looked at the papers he had found in the glovebox. The owner of the car was from Mount Vernon. It was one county over.

Bone called Sheriff Musgrove trying to find more information.

"Don, this is Sheriff Bone, out of Wayne County. I have a suspicious death here and found the paperwork to the owner of the car. Are you familiar with Linda Tullis?"

"Hell, that girl has been missing for over a year. Her daughter, Jenny, too. The mother used to come up here every day looking for information. I don't know where she is now. I think the mother lost everything trying to find her daughter. It was a sad situation. Where are you exactly? I think I will drive over to see everything first-hand," Don said. "It will take me an hour to get there."

144

"We'll be here. You might want one of your boys to start trying to locate the mother. We're going to need her, and she needs to know before this is blasted out on the news."

Bone saw the state police roll in and went to share their findings. "Morning. I'm Captain Paris. What do you have?"

Bone walked him to the scene. "Has anyone touched anything?"

"No, I taped off the scene. They have been clearing this land for the last month."

The men walked to where Sam was. After introductions and explanations of why and how the body had been discovered, the captain wanted to know who everyone was. Notes were taken, and he surveyed the property. Crime scene notes were jotted down along the way. He made a crime scene sketch of the car and bodies.

Two other state troopers arrived. Captain Paris stated, "I need you to bag and label the evidence. This is a fragile scene, with deteriorated bodies. I will need pictures. The mortician is here. Please assist him in getting the body ready for transport, and maintain the chain of custody."

Violet shared the history of the owners. She said, "I was informed by the wife of Bart that he had killed a neighbor some time ago. It was hearsay, but this might be worth looking into."

Then, Sam told Don, "Johnny, the son of Bart, stated he killed his father. I haven't seen Bart since that time. Johnny is in prison. Sheriff Bone can tell you more about that. You may want to bring in the dogs and a search team."

Sheriff Musgrove, from Mount Vernon, arrived and went straight to the scene of the bodies. Sheriff Bone walked over to provide an update. Musgrove shared a file with him on the missing person report. The car was hers.

Steve Tolliver, Medical Examiner, introduced himself to the state troopers and offered them gloves. The body bags were taken to the scene, along with identification tags. With the assistance of the state troopers, measurements were taken, and the bodies were bagged. Photos were taken, and diagrams were marked. Inventory

145

was taken and documented. Evidence was recorded with location, time of collection, and labeled. The bodies were removed from the site.

Captain Paris instructed his troopers to bag anything in the car, take pictures, label, and secure contents. Photographs were taken of the entire property at that point. Documentation was completed on who had discovered the bodies, as well as the circumstances.

Captain Paris did a scene debriefing with all of the officials involved. He then called his office and shared the findings. "I will need a team to canvas the land for bodies as well as get cadaver dogs out here immediately. The dogs will be vital at this point. You would understand if you saw this property. I will get started on visual clues."

Sheriff Musgrove asked Captain Paris, "Do I need to bring in some more of my boys from Mount Vernon? They can be here in thirty minutes."

"Yes, and Sheriff Bone, I need you to do the same. As soon as they get here, let me know. We have a huge task at hand here."

One hour later, twelve men and three dogs were on site.

"Listen up," shouted Captain Paris. "I need you to work the land in groups of three. That leaves us four teams. You will start at the current scene at the north side of the property and work your way to the tree line on the south side of the property. You will be looking for disturbed vegetation, disturbed soil, compaction of soil that looks like a grave, and also depressions in the soil. Anything that looks odd is worth looking at closer. We will have to move all junk that is on this property. You never know what it is covering. Any questions?"

The teams dispersed.

Sam was irritated by the excess audio stimulation. Sirens wailed as more cars rolled in. The barking of the dogs was rubbing Sam's nerves raw. He was used to a quiet, tranquil life, and that's how he wanted to keep it.

Three hours later, the body of Bart was found. One of the officers blew his whistle, and everyone came running.

"This looked like a depressed grave with minimal vegetation growing. A body was partially exposed. An old sink, wash tub, and empty containers were strewn on top of it," said Deputy Jones. Sheriff Bone called the coroner.

"I'll need you to return to the location you just left. We have another body."

The same process was established as before. Bart's wallet was still in his pants. Johnny was in prison but would need to be questioned. Sheriff Bone said, "Johnny is mentally compromised and talks to himself. He is deranged, but we can make an attempt to question him. Johnny was abused and beaten all his life. He hated his father."

The entire property was taped off. At dusk, the incoming officers were briefed. Captain Paris announced, "We will need flashlights and spotlights to complete the remainder of our search." Officers left to retrieve the items.

That night at Sam's place, there was a feeling of weariness. Violet and Sara had returned home after being questioned. Dinner was a somber event. C.W., Sam, and Sullivan had shared everything, including finding Bart's body. It was closure, but it created a sadness as well. Johnny would be in prison for life now. He had admitted to killing his father.

"I know they will find Mary's husband on that property. I just pray there isn't another dozen bodies that are discovered."

C.W. spoke up. "Well, Sullivan, it looks like we need to bless the land. This is a little more than what I bargained for."

"You got that right. Now I want to remove everything as fast as possible and clear the land. It's downright scary. I'm afraid to plow the fields. Might plow up some bodies. I didn't know them, but you did, and they lived down the road. No telling what else they will find," Sullivan declared.

Everyone turned in early. C.W. and Sullivan were going to farm tomorrow. Only Sam was going to the property.

Sara thought about the girl and her child all night. At breakfast, she couldn't keep quiet any longer. "I have to know more about this girl and the child. Her mother would not leave if she thought there was any chance her daughter would return. The mother did not believe Linda was dead, therefore, she would never leave the place Linda called home. Sheriff Musgrove stated she was at the police station every day for months. Then, her homestead went into foreclosure, she lost the car, her job, and then she disappeared. I want to go to their home. Sheriff Musgrove gave me directions, and I can find it. I have to do it."

Violet spoke softly. "I know how distraught you are after finding them. I think you feel a responsibility. If you have to go, I'll go with you."

"Thank you, Grandma."

Sam immediately spoke up. "I believe I would like to go. Sheriff Bone doesn't need me. I just felt Mary might need us for support. I'll have Pearline stay with her. Finding Linda's mother is more important. Let's get ready."

Sara went to her father and hugged him. "This is very important to me, Dad. I can only imagine the pain and sorrow she must feel over losing her daughter. Now we know she lost a lot more. We need to find and help this mother." Sara walked away pondering her thoughts and the events from the past. Sara realized she was doing exactly what she was meant to do. Help others.

They left for Mount Vernon thirty minutes later. The drive was short, and they pulled into an old farm that sat in the middle of acreage. Fields surrounded the house. The basic, two-story respectable picturesque home stood silently, as though waiting for life again. It was supposedly vacant, yet the flowers that surrounded the house looked well-tended.

They parked in front of a ramshackle doghouse. The low, white picket fence looked freshly painted.

148

"Doesn't that seem odd, Dad? No one lives here, but the fence has a fresh coat of paint, and the flowers are well kept. It's like someone is still maintaining the farm."

"I agree," Sam replied. "Be on the alert. We are going to look everywhere and under everything. She may be sick or desperate. Maybe she has given up. Let's walk to the house together. We appear to be a family and less threatening than a bill collector or the police."

As they walked on the sidewalks, the steps revealed two red flowerpots with Dahlias in them. They stepped onto the newly painted front porch and looked over the property facing the front of the house. Nothing moved.

Sam knocked. There was no answer, so he knocked louder. He looked in the window with Sara and Violet. Violet said, "The house is clean and still taken care of. The decorations are warm and have importance to whomever lives here."

Sam tried the water well manual pump, and it worked well. He went to the back door and peered in. The kitchen was cozy in hues of blue. Sam knocked again. He turned and walked to the barn that was well maintained. As he entered, he thought he heard rustling in the loft. Sam started talking. "My name is Sam. My daughter and mother-in-law are here with me. This morning we discovered news about Linda and Jenny. We wanted to tell you about it. Sheriff Musgrove told us about you going to the police station daily for over a year. He came here yesterday to talk to you. Please come and talk to us."

Sam turned and walked out to go to the small building at the back of the property. There in the two-room shed lay a woman. Her hair was jet black, and her lips were reddish blue. Sam saw how thin she was. It was devastating to see veins prominent and bones protruding. He waved for Violet and Sara to come, then put his finger to his lips for them to be quiet. Sam stepped out of the shed.

"I'm not sure there is a good way to wake her. She is ill. Look at her bones and skin. It reminds me of Pearl when she was dying," he choked out. Tears were in his eyes. Violet entered the shed with Sara. They saw exactly why he was distraught. This person wasn't just thin, she was skeletal. Her gauntness was from lack of food.

Violet walked to her cot and sat on the wooden chair by her.

"Mrs. Tullis," she said quietly. Violet feared she was close to dying. Again, Violet said, louder, "Mrs. Tullis." There was the slightest of movement. "Sara, go to the car and get the snacks we brought. She is starving."

Sara returned with the drinks and food. Violet put her hand on Mrs. Tullis' arm and gently patted it.

Marie awoke, startled and disoriented. She said, "I'm going. I just wanted to be sure everything was in order. I fed the cat. I'm not doing anything wrong." She realized Violet was sitting in front of her and tried to jump up. She was too weak to go far. Sara handed her a bottle of orange juice and half a sandwich. She grabbed at the food and sat back down and ate slowly.

Violet started, "My name is Violet. This is Sara, my granddaughter. My son-in-law is by the door. We mean you no harm. Can you tell us your name?"

"Marie, it's Marie Tullis. What do you want?"

"Do you live here? It's a beautiful place and well maintained. Your flowers are delightful."

As though in a daze, Marie started rambling. "I've lived here for thirty years farming with my husband. He died ten years ago. My daughter and granddaughter lived here with us. Linda was such a help, and Jenny such a delight. I couldn't farm, so we rented the farmland out to farmers. It was for practically nothing. They wanted to take advantage of me, knowing they could. I had a huge garden every year, and Linda and I canned for weeks on end. We had chickens, too." Marie reached for the cookie Sara was holding as well as the other half of the sandwich. Sara smiled and released them.

"My daughter and Jenny went to pick up some canning supplies that were really cheap. We really needed more, as the canning kept us going all winter. They were for sale on a bulletin board at the hardware store. She never returned. I have looked for her every day for over a year. I lost everything. My farm went into foreclosure, but I came back and stayed here in the shed. I knew Linda would come back here if she could."

"I know it's been hard for you to go through this ordeal by yourself," Violet said. "We live in Wayne County. Have you been there?"

Marie nodded her head to acknowledge as she kept eating.

"There isn't a good way to say what we came her to share with you. We've been clearing land we just bought and found your daughter and granddaughter. The police are investigating, as their deaths are under strange circumstances."

Marie started sobbing as she rocked back and forth. Sam and Sara were both crying silently.

After a few minutes, Violet got up and spoke to Sam quietly. "She's not going to want to go to a hospital. What do you suggest we do? The houses haven't been built yet for the workers. We can't leave her here."

"We'll have to help her gather her things and take her with us. I can stay at your house with C.W. and Sullivan. She can have my room. She needs a lot of care. Dr. Gerstein needs to be notified and come to see her immediately. You know what to do, Violet."

Violet nodded her head. Sara was sitting beside Marie consoling her.

Violet returned to Marie's side. "Marie, how do you feel about coming home with us? We'll bring you back here after you are better and have some strength. Dr. Gerstein is a good friend of mine, and you need medical attention. Would you rather go to a hospital?"

"No, I'm not going to a hospital. I'd be more alone than I am now." Marie attempted to stand several times, but her legs were too weak. Sam came to her side.

"I'll carry you to the car. My name is Sam. We'll help you get better, and then we'll help you get to wherever you want to go, or you can stay on with us. It's your decision." Sam slipped his arm under her legs and lifted her effortlessly. He placed her in the back seat beside Violet. Is there anything you want to take with us? I'll get it for you," Sam said.

"I need the bags under the cot, and I can't leave the kitten. It's by itself now and will die."

Sam smiled. "Good thing Sara has way too many cats, so this one will fit in perfectly." He went to get her belongings. Sara searched for the cat. It was a beautiful, small tabby. Sara held it close all the way home. As they drove, Marie had her head on Violet's shoulder. Sam carried Marie to his room and placed her in his bed.

"I really can't take your bed. I can sleep on the floor," Marie said to Sam.

"No, I can sleep at Violet's other house on the back of the property. Two of my best friends are there. You need to be here for Violet and Sara to care for. She already has Dr. Gerstein coming. You can meet the rest of our family later. You need to eat and get stronger, then I will show you the farm. There's no rush in you leaving or making decisions. Just rest and get better," Sam encouraged. He knew she wanted more information about Linda and Jenny's death, but this wasn't the time.

Dr. Gerstein arrived and assessed Marie. Blood was drawn for a baseline. He and Sara started intravenous fluids with vitamins and told Sara to run them for the next twenty-four hours. He gave Marie a B-12 injection as well.

Sara went to the kitchen and threw vegetables and some cooked beef together for a pot of soup. Marie nodded off quickly. Everyone gathered around the kitchen table. Sara said, "This is one of the hardest things I have ever dealt with. After finding the bodies and now Marie, I feel a loss myself."

"We all do," Sam replied. "It brings back old memories and new trauma in regards to all that has happened."

CHAPTER 26

C.W. and Sullivan walked in and sat down. Sam shared the events of the day.

"C.W., I thought things were going to quiet down now that you're farming. Boy, was I wrong! Did you find anything else on the property today?"

"No, and we only have one acre left to search. Maybe it will all be over. Looks like we need to start building as soon as we can. I'm going to need a crew for quick progress."

"I think there's enough farmers and their families right here surrounding us that could handle a few extra dollars. Pearline knows more folks in Mill Shoals, so I'll give her a call, and they can contact me. We'll get this organized and started quickly. First, we need to haul off the junk. We have to farm the rest of the week. I'm sure that in two days there will be some hired help to clear the land. We will need a couple of trailers, so plan on buying those this week, C.W." He turned to Sullivan. "How do you feel about going to town and getting the building supplies? You've done construction before, so this should be easy for you," Sam said.

Sullivan nodded. "No problem. I can handle the construction side, C.W. We need to walk off the property and decide where we're building so I can measure and get supplies. I think we need to build the barn first. We're going to have too much sitting out and no way to protect it."

"Sounds good," C.W. responded. "Sara, I need input from you and Violet regarding the housing, the cooking area, and everything you want. We need to get everything discussed and make sure we do it right the first time."

"I'll get with Grandma, and I will draw out how we think the cooking area should be designed," Sara said. "This is going to be a business, so we need to plan it out well in case we need to expand. We need an area for washers and dryers. Yes, more than one, or we will never get clothes clean. This will take the burden off Grandma. We need a new washer and dryer here for her as well."

CHAPTER 27

Sam got up and went to look in on Marie. She had touched him.
Violet and Sara realized he was having flashbacks of Pearl in her
final days. Sam always was a caring soul.

Marie recovered quickly with everyone doting on her. The intravenous fluids were completed, and she was now joining everyone at
mealtime. She even started carrying in the vegetables and washing
some dishes.

C.W. and Sullivan met her briefly. Marie walked to the garage
where she could see Sam working. "Would you mind taking me to
where you found Jenny?" Marie asked Sam.

"I can do that. You know we don't know the circumstances."
Sam pointed to a chair for Marie to sit in, then proceeded to tell
Marie about Bart and Johnny. "Bart killed his wife years ago." Sam
didn't leave out who they had assaulted over the years. "You need to
know Johnny was mentally ill. He went to prison after he assaulted
Sara. They stayed to themselves, so no one would have known he
was killing people. I'm so sorry, Marie." Sam reached forward and
took Marie's hand. "No one should have to go through this. Especially, not these devastating circumstances."

"Somewhere in the back of my mind, I knew they wouldn't be coming home. I knew something had happened. I am grateful to know the truth. Now, will you take me around your property and to where you found her?" Marie asked quietly.

"Do you feel up to walking, or would you rather drive?" Sam asked.

"I'd like to walk. It's a nice day. Tell me about you and everybody here," Marie said.

As they headed to the back of the property, Sam shared his war experiences and how Pearl had passed away. "We call this Lover's Lane. I made it when I first married Pearl. This is the graveyard for the family, including Pearl." He pointed to her headstone. They walked past the pond and headed towards what had once been Medlar's property. As they got to the property line, Sam went down the bank and reached back for Marie's hand to help her down. They crossed the road, and Marie saw Linda's car. She walked to it quickly. Sam followed.

Captain Paris was completing the final day of searching. He walked to the car, and Sam introduced them. It was a solemn moment. Paris asked, "When did your daughter go missing?"

Marie gave him the date and explained what Linda had been going to do that day.

"They were found in the car," Sam shared. "Jenny was in the back seat, and Linda was in the trunk. I can hardly say it, as I know it must hurt you to see this car again knowing the facts."

Marie started sobbing, and Sam put his arm around her to comfort her. It was too emotional for any words. Marie walked around the car and looked in it, as well as in the trunk. Sam could only imagine what she was thinking and the pain they had suffered.

"We found Bart's body last week, and we are still looking for Mary's husband. Bart's wife shared with Violet that Bart had killed him, and he was never seen again."

It was like a horror movie when the whistles rang out over the field. The last two officers had found a depressed area on the far side of the creek. The routine started again. Sam went to Marie. "Let's get you back to the house. This is not where you need to be right now."

Marie went to lie down.

"Violet, I need you to call Pearline and be ready. I'll pick them up in the car. Let Pearline know what's happening, so Mary is aware she will need to identify her husband."

They were waiting on Sam in the driveway. "Are you okay, Mary?" Sam asked quietly.

"Yes, Sam. I knew this day would come. I accepted it months ago. He would have come home if he could have. We were together fifty years."

The body was exhumed. Identification was in the grave site. The coroner took the body away. Mary handled everything well.

"Why don't you come to the house for a while? We need to talk about plans for the burial."

"Thank you, Sam," Mary said. Sam saw tears in her eyes. Pearline had her arm around Mary. The trauma these last few weeks had been overwhelming. Now, the burial would be closure, but still traumatic.

Violet hurried to Mary and hugged her.

"I'm okay, Violet," she said. "It's not like I wasn't waiting on this day."

Everyone sat at the table. Marie came also and told Mary how sorry she was for her loss. Mary said the same to Marie as she took her hand and squeezed it. As they sat around the table, Violet asked an important question. "We have to make a decision about where you want to bury your husband, Mary. Marie, you will need to decide as well. You are more than welcome to use our family cemetery. It is ultimately your decision."

Mary spoke first. "I can still have him close if I bury him on your property. Are you sure you don't mind?"

"It would be fine to bury him here." They set about making plans.

Marie was quiet. "I don't know what to do," she said softly. This isn't something you plan for. I don't know what's going to happen

157

to me. I am so lost right now." Tears were falling. Sam gently put an arm around her.

"You have time to think about it. In the meantime, I'll tell you about our plans here. We are building housing for all the workers. Maybe you would want to stay on a while and heal. It will be a paying job. You will have an opportunity to get on your feet again," Sam said.

Marie nodded.

Sara joined Marie at the table. She shared the details of the courtyard, the kitchen area, the living arrangements, and so much more. Violet came and sat beside Pearline. "Ladies, we have to decide how we can make this canning business work. Not only will we sell the canned products, we will also give to the needy."

They decided an L-shaped table in the covered courtyard would be efficient in an assembly line. "We need a large stove with lots of counter space. The labels would be the final step."

Marie asked, "What tasks are required in the process?"

They then discussed the roadside fruit and vegetable stand. Who would man it? Where would it be and how many? Mary and Marie both had excellent ideas. It was a welcome relief to think of something else besides the funerals. It was actually hope—hope that they would start over and find happiness within themselves again.

Sara completed the drawing for that part of the business. Then, the discussion went to the housing for the workers. All the women felt the houses needed to have bathrooms, kitchens, bedrooms, and living rooms. Then, they discussed how to achieve these goals.

Dinner that Sunday was buffet style, and everyone grabbed a plate. It was a working dinner. Sara handed her drawings to C.W.

"We all had an input on how to make everything work efficiently. We kept the housing small, but functional. Washers and dryers will be in a washroom, holding multiple sets. The kitchen will be twice the size of this one, and we drew the layout. We also want an outside fire pit for grilling and smoking. I hope this helps. You will see an

L-shaped workstation to turn the products out faster. This way, we can have workers on both sides of the counter for efficiency."

C.W. looked at the drawing as Sullivan and Sam stood looking over his shoulder. "Great job, ladies. I think we can manage this. Sullivan, now we can determine what we are building first. I know you recommended the barn first, and I agree. Let's do some measuring and get some lumber," C.W. suggested.

Sam said, "I have seven men so far that have experience building. One younger man isn't so experienced, but I can see he is destitute, and he can be our gopher. Plus, we can develop him and show him how to do carpentry work, farm, and maybe run the roadside stands."

"This is all coming together," Sullivan said. "Let's stake the housing out as well as the barn. Then, when that is complete, we'll work on our houses."

"Absolutely, we got this," C.W. replied. The men went to the property and started planning for construction.

Sara walked to the property later to find her dad. The men were measuring in the location they had chosen for the barn. "Can I interrupt you for a minute?" Sara asked. "I know we haven't talked much about Marie, but I think we need to see if she wants her daughter's car fixed so she can drive it. Linda's dad gave it to her two years ago. Marie may want it."

Sam looked surprised. "Sara, I hadn't even thought about the car and what to do with it. You have a good thought there. We just need to clean it up and do some maintenance on it. We know it was running well before all this happened."

"I think we can all help," Sullivan said, "and it won't take long at all. We need to scrub the trunk and back seat. The car has been open for several weeks now. Sam, why don't you talk to Marie about it before we start anything?"

"Okay, I can do that tonight."

"One other thing," Sara stated. "Can you ask her about her farm that is in foreclosure? How much would it cost to get it back to her, and does she want it back. Maybe we could get it cheap and pay for it with the money C.W. has given us, and she can live on it or sell it. What do you think?"

C.W. smiled. "You have a heart of gold, Sara. You always think of others. She has been through a lot, and I think when we get answers to those questions, we can help however we need to." C.W. hugged her.

"Last, but not least, we need to bury the three bodies. Maybe this weekend for closure. Mary's husband also. This would put closure on everything, and maybe it will help give them relief to move on."

"I know you're right," Sam replied. "I'll tread lightly and ask Marie if she decided on our cemetery."

Sara walked back to the farm and shared with Violet their conversation. Mary and Pearline were getting ready to walk home. Violet quietly said, "We are planning a funeral this weekend."

Marie walked in about that time. "Will I still have the opportunity to bury Linda and Jenny here, too?"

"Of course," Violet responded. "We want to help both of you in any way we can. It's important to finalize the plans and say our goodbyes. You will see them again in heaven. It's important to enjoy the time you have with family and remember the great times."

They both agreed on the family cemetery. Sara called the funeral home and made the arrangements. Johnny had admitted to the murders and even gave gory details. Therefore, the bodies had been released. Sara got with both women and helped write the eulogy for their loved ones.

When the men returned to the house, Sara shared their plans for a funeral Saturday at 10 a.m. She asked Sullivan to pick up flowers when he went to get the lumber.

Sam was relieved he wouldn't have to ask those questions. He saw Marie working in the flowerbed and asked her to go for a walk.

"Marie, I know the funeral is Saturday. I wanted to ask you about the car and what you want to do with it. I know it was given to Linda in love, and we thought you might want to keep it. C.W. and

Sullivan agreed they want to help get it ready to drive, if that's what you want. I know it's a big decision, under these circumstances."

"I think I would like that," Marie responded. "I know it sounds morbid, but that's okay. I can deal with that. It will let me keep a part of them with me."

Sam continued. "What about the farm? If you could, would you want to return and stay there? Would you sell it, if you still owned it?"

"I wish I owned it. Then I would sell it to have a nest egg. I don't have anything and am depending on your family's kindness. I wouldn't live there again, but I would love to have the furniture and different things that have good memories for me," Marie said. "I plan to stay on here and help with the canning and gardening. I love gardening and, of course, my favorite is tending the flowers."

"You definitely have a green thumb," Sam said.

"I have to move out of your bedroom. It's not right that I take that from you after all you and your family have done for me."

"No, don't worry about that. I am good in the other house and can horse around with the guys." Sam squeezed her hand.

Marie rose on tiptoes and kissed Sam on the cheek. "Thank you, Sam."

He nodded. They walked back to the house with answers to everything—well, almost everything. Sam was having some odd feelings that he didn't want to think about right then.

The funeral was solemn, but it was definitely closure. C.W. and Sullivan had prepared the graves, and the flowers were beautiful. The tears came from the relief that it was over and done.

It was a solemn procession back to the house. Pearline announced, "I asked Mary to stay on at my house. I enjoy having someone there. In just a little while, we'll both be busy with canning and other things."

Mary nodded. "I'm grateful and have made a lifelong friend. I'm looking forward to staying busy with the new business venture."

CHAPTER 28

Willis came to the farm early Monday morning. Sara could tell he had been crying.

"What's wrong, Willis?" Sara asked, as she put her arms around him.

"Dad had a heart attack. He didn't make it."

Sam was devastated. "Oh no. Mark didn't tell me he was sick." Sam put his arms around Willis and gave him a hug. "What can I do? I'm so sorry."

"Can I bury him in the cemetery? I want him close. He wasn't sick. Just one of those freak things."

"Of course, I would want you to. I'll help you with everything," Sam offered.

"Sara, I inherited the farm. I don't know what to do. This changes everything. My brother wants to join the army. I'm responsible for the animals, the farming, and the upkeep. Would you be disappointed if we move to my farm instead of your grandmother's homestead? Of course, that's when we get married. I'll remodel everything just like you wanted." Willis sat down on the steps feeling despair. He rested his head in his hands and cried.

"Honey, I just want to be with you. We'll talk about what we want to do. Right now, we have to work through your father's death. I am so sorry. I know what loss is," Sara said gently.

All the neighbors showed up for the funeral. They walked through Lover's Lane to the cemetery. This unexpected death was more emotional. Willis and his brother spoke of a loving father, and Sam spoke of a lifelong friendship. He would be missed. This chain of events would affect Sara and Willis and their plans.

The following Monday, the workers arrived, and the barn went up quickly. It was huge. The homeless boy was Todd Simpson. C.W. and Sullivan noticed he didn't leave when the other workers did and figured out his situation. C.W. asked Todd, "Do you have anywhere to go for the night?"

"No. I've been finding odd jobs. I sleep anywhere I can get a roof over my head. My parents died in a car wreck two years ago. I don't have any family now."

Sullivan and C.W. just looked at each other. "When the living quarters are done, you can have the first one. In the meantime, Violet won't mind if you eat with us. For now, I will bring the cot and sleeping bag from the garage, and you are welcome to stay in the barn. That way you can keep an eye on things."

Todd looked at C.W. and Sullivan. "Thank you for allowing me to stay. I'll do whatever I can to earn my worth. Maybe I'll be able to pay you back for your kindness and generosity one day."

Sullivan slapped Todd on the back. They all drove to Violet's for dinner.

C.W. stated, "I want you to meet Todd Simpson. He will have one of the houses we build. Hope you don't mind another mouth to feed."

Violet smiled. "We love having you, Todd. Make yourself at home. The family is growing daily."

Sam walked through the field to find Sullivan and C.W. They both saw him as he came through the backyard of Violet's farm. "Hey, Sam," C.W. called out. "What's going on?"

"I was hoping you both could help me get Marie's daughter's car scrubbed out. Then, we can determine what we need to replace. She said she wants to keep it for sentimental reasons. The outside is spotless."

Sullivan responded first. "I looked at it a few weeks back. The car runs but needs plugs. We can scrub everything. When do you want to get started?"

Sam replied, "We have to move it to the barn for water access, so whenever you guys are ready. Marie wishes she still had her farm to sell for some cash flow. Do you think we could use some of our money and pay it off for her? I don't think the foreclosure has gone through yet."

"I think that's what we should do," C.W. said in agreement. "We need to help her move on. I know having a little money would make her feel different about herself. Then, having a car again would be the icing on the cake."

"I know. I know you saw her when we first brought her here. It's night and day now. She put on weight and has some color. She even laughs now. I thought she was going to die. Brought back some bad memories," Sam shared.

Sam and C.W. walked away from the house. "I know what you're referring to, Sam. I think Marie is a nice woman. It's okay to care about someone. It's been years since Pearl passed. Take your time and get to know her. She is a kind person. We all see it. She looks at you as a man, not just her rescuer, Sam. You may want to take a chance."

"What would I say to Violet and Sara? It feels right, but it feels wrong. It's like, I'm doing something wrong," Sam said, anxiously.

164

"I understand, Sam. Violet and Sara will be happy for you. They see how she looks at you. It's all right. You'll eventually find the right time to bring it up to them. Take a breath and live."

"Okay, let's get this car cleaned up. That's a start," Sam said. Together, they moved the car and stripped and cleaned it from top to bottom. There was no evidence there had been so much trauma surrounding it. They talked about Todd and the other farmers who were helping them build the living quarters.

"Everything is coming together. Todd is a good worker and grateful for a home. All the farmers have skills, and our progress has been amazing. I'm leaving the floor of the old barn where it is. I think I'll put some benches out for seating. It would be nice to have a fire some time and a place to sit and enjoy it. It seems like the drama from the past is over," C.W. said.

"It's about time. I want everything to be calm and serene for a while. Unfortunately, I am worried about Willis. He seems depressed," Sam said. "I can see Sara moving to his farm eventually and staying with him. I'm okay with that. Willis is going to need some help. Can you think of anybody to help him work the farm?"

At the same time, they both said, "Todd."

"He may be young, but he's got mechanical skills and is a hard worker. I'll talk to Willis and Sara to see what they want to do," Sam said. "Maybe you could feel Todd out and see if he would rather stay with you. He may not want to go to Willis'. He's happy here. You can see it in his face."

"I'll check it out," C.W. said. They both started their chores for the day.

It turns out neither one had to say anything to Todd. At Sunday dinner, Sara invited Willis. After everyone had started eating, Sara announced, "I feel I need to plan on how to remodel Willis' house. Todd and I spoke earlier this week, and he's willing to stay at Willis' until we get the ranch house completed or he decides what he wants to do. He is willing to help all of us any way he can. Right now, we have to keep the farm going."

Todd smiled and nodded his head. "I'll help everyone with anything you need. You have been so good to me. I feel like I have a big family now."

Willis spoke quietly. "I hope it is all right with everyone that we invited Todd to stay and help us farm. He can help build or do anything else you want him to. I just can't do this by myself, and Sara is going back to the hospital to work next week. The house is pretty run down, and the yard needs some work also."

Marie chimed in. "I'll come tend to your yard tomorrow. I love working in the yard. Do you have tools? I can mow, too. I would love to do that, since I have the yard here pretty much done. I can do that one day every week."

"The yard and flowers are beautiful thanks to you, Marie. I think it would be great if you want to help them out," Violet agreed.

"We'll all help you remodel when you decide what you want done," Sam shared. "That will make it go faster. We can upgrade inside and out. Just let us know when you are ready. I'll come by later today, and we will see what needs to be a priority. Between us all, we can decide how to get it done. We are family, and we will help each other always."

C.W. and Sullivan nodded in agreement.

The weeks and months flew by. The housing was completed. Ten small houses were connected. Each had its own bathroom, kitchen, and a combined living area. It was a secure setting. The courtyard had its new fountain. The cooking area was huge, with an outside pit, tables, and grilling area. Mary decided to stay on with Pearline. Todd stayed on at Willis' farm. Marie was still at the house with Violet and Sam. "Who the hell is going to live in the housing we just built?" C.W. said, laughing.

"Well, I'll stay in one until my house is built," Sullivan said. "I think we have to look at who in the surrounding county may be barely making it. Maybe they would want to sell their land and live here for free. I'm sure some of the older farmers would find that appealing. Sam said they needed extra money, and the men showed up to build the barn. Let's just put it out there to all of the farmers helping us and see what happens. We may find some more farmland to buy. We need a cook for the workers, too. We need someone to do the laundry. We have three older women who can, but we need people to tend to the garden, canning, and the roadside stands. We have a lot to do and need more hands on deck. I'm sure some of these farmers have family and friends that need the money."

"You're a good businessman," C.W. said. "Let's get Violet to pull together a meeting with the women, so we can have everyone's input. Those women can tell the world in nothing flat."

The following day, everyone met at the property and looked at the layout. Marie announced, "I can be over the garden. The garden will need to be huge in order to achieve what we are talking about. I need two young men for tilling, planting, watering, and bringing the food in for canning or to sell. I can still manage the flowers and yard at Sam's and Willis'."

Pearline, Mary, and Violet had already talked about the canning and who would do each step of the process. "We have the canning process down and a system already in place. We will need to purchase more canning jars and lids." Violet mentioned the jars at the old farm weren't there. Sam just smiled remembering where they were buried and what was in them. Those would be discovered later.

"Most likely, we will need two to three more women to help us," Violet said. "It may be feasible to have one of them at the food stand as well. If we have one stand at the crossroads and one stand at the fresh market in town on Saturdays, we will narrow down the need for extra hands. We all just have to be flexible and able to do all the duties as needed.

"Everything will be seasonal. As each crop ripens, we sell it or can it. It will be trial and error this year. Neighbors will tell others of what we're doing, and we will see everyone come to us eventually. At that point, we can sell eggs, honey, and more."

"I see a plan coming together." Sam smiled. "Eventually, we may want farm animals if we find someone to slaughter and process. That can be a discussion for the future. Corn, beans, and wheat will be a focus for the farming. I think this venture will help everyone, and no one will go hungry or be without a home."

Everyone agreed. The ball was in play, and a business was established. Maybe not the normal business, but one of caring for others while you still make a living. Sam looked at everyone who was a part of their next venture in life. "The Lord will provide whatever we need as long as we care for others."

Everyone looked at Sam and, in unison, said, "AMEN."

CHAPTER 29

The days flew by. The seasons changed as well as the crops. One Saturday morning, Sam was up extremely early. Violet was in the garden, and Sam approached to help.

"I can see you like the first worm, too," Sam joked.

"Well, there's never a dull moment here anymore. I love it. Everyone has their duties, and the business is excelling thanks to everyone and their skills. Everyone is working hard. Sam, can we talk a minute?" Violet pointed to the benches under the old oak tree.

"Of course, Violet. I always have time for you." Sam was fearful of the conversation that he felt was coming. He would never hurt Violet or anyone else intentionally.

"Sam, I can see you care for Marie. She just beams when you are around. I want you to know I have no issues with you starting a life with Marie. Pearl has been gone a long time. We will always love her, and no one can take our memories of her. You have been single now for over twenty years. You have a chance to start a new life with a wonderful woman. I think the world of Marie, and so does Sara. I want you to know if you decide to have a permanent relationship with Marie, you are more than welcome to live in mine and Ezra's home. Best of all, C.W., Sullivan, and you have it remodeled. They

169

can move to the houses they just completed. It's like musical chairs. Everyone just moves to the next house that comes open."

Violet and Sam laughed, but Sam took the conversation seriously.

"Violet, it's too early for me to make that decision. I enjoy Marie, and I'm fond of her. I'm not sure where we're going with this, but I will take to heart our conversation. I want you to know, I'm not really comfortable with it all. My honor is to you and Sara and always will be."

"I know that. Don't put your life on hold too long. Sara will marry soon and probably have babies. You have my blessing," Violet said, with fondness.

"I have a lot to work through," Sam replied. "I love you like a mother and a friend. I have emotions that this is Pearl's home and your home. It doesn't feel right to bring another woman in as my wife, lover, or whatever. I stay busy, and I'm happy. My feelings for Marie are due to compassion for her situation. It's not time for me to make a decision so serious. Most important, the love Pearl and I shared will stay in this heart forever. I was privileged to share her life and our beautiful Sara. Those we truly love live forever in our hearts."

"I understand, Sam. If things change, you have my blessing."

"Thanks, Violet."

Sam took some of the tomatoes, and they headed to the house.

CHAPTER 30

Sara was deep into her work as a nurse at the hospital, but she always made time for the people who surrounded their farm and lives. Now, Willis was her priority. He had to heal from losing his father. Their life was different now. He intoxicated her with his hands, his breath on hers, and his very being. Willis was her true love.

Sara worked late, then went to Willis'. She found him coming out of the shower.

"What a wonderful way to meet me," Sara said, flirting. She lay her head on his bare chest.

Willis ran his fingers through her hair. His breath caressed her forehead as he tilted her head back and gazed into her eyes. His hair was wet, but his body was an inferno. Passion gripped her as she listened to their hearts beat. Then, the warmth of his breath touched her ear, and she felt herself mold her body to his.

He removed her blouse as his mouth covered hers. They were passionate for each other. Her uniform dropped to the floor as he pulled her to the bed and left no space between them as their legs entwined. Their mouths and tongues teased each other to a carnal place they were both seeking. Sara wanted everything and more.

Their mouths pressed together, and a violent hunger seized them both. They were in the moment, with no thoughts of anything but each other's pleasure.

Sara melted into Willis and let him consume her totally. The wetness of his mouth on her breasts was stirring her to a place she had wanted for so long. His hands caressed her breast and traveled down her abdomen to her thighs. Then, his tongue, blazing with heat, aroused a fire in her. At that moment, there was simply response.

Sara touched and stroked him in search of release. A cry came from him as he thrust deeper, and they were both spinning, yearning, and demanding of each other as climatic ripples tore through them both.

His coal black eyes looked at her with love as she curled against him. He drew her close, and they slept entwined.

Sara woke late the following day. The bed was empty.

"Hey, there you are," Sara said to Willis, finding him in the kitchen.

"Morning, honey, just making coffee for us," Willis said, smiling.

"I thought you were already in the field." Sara walked to him. Willis stood perfectly still, admiring everything about her. He was smiling at her seductively.

Willis wrapped his arms tightly around her. "Great things are to come for us," Willis whispered to her. He pulled a small velvet box from his pocket and stepped back.

"Your dad gave me your mother's wedding ring. He thought you would love to wear it as my wife. He knew I was going to ask you to marry me."

Sara took a deep breath as he opened the dainty box. Inside was the beautiful diamond ring that had been tucked away in her father's belongings for years.

"Oh, Willis. This means so much to me."

"Marry me, Sara?"

Sara went into his arms and snuggled in for the long journey. "Yes. Forever. It's time for a new chapter in life. The old traumas are gone. This life now, is a new beginning for so many people and all our lives are blessed."

ACKNOWLEDGEMENTS

A very special thank you to Gary Westfal for guiding me through this awesome journey.

Thank you to Stephanee Killen of Integrative Ink for her direction in completing *Chasing Justice*. The knowledge I gained is priceless.

CPSIA information can be obtained
at www.ICGtesting.com
Printed in the USA
BVHW071154271222
655045BV00004B/48

9 781737 801009